WITH EVERY BREATH

A LIGHT MY FIRE SERIES NOVEL

J.H. CROIX

This is a work of fiction. Names, characters, businesses, places, events and incidents are either the products of the author's imagination or used in a fictitious manner. Any resemblance to actual persons, living or dead, or actual events is purely coincidental.

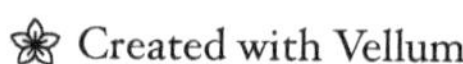 Created with Vellum

To finding light to guide us through darkness.

Sign up for my newsletter for information on new releases & get a FREE copy of one of my books!

http://jhcroixauthor.com/subscribe/

Follow me!
jhcroix@jhcroix.com
https://amazon.com/author/jhcroix
https://www.bookbub.com/authors/j-h-croix
https://www.facebook.com/jhcroix
https://www.instagram.com/jhcroix/

Chapter One

ALICE

I stood at the edge of the lake with my boots planted on the dock. Taking a breath, I inhaled the crisp mountain air. Home. I was *home*.

My eyes arced across the lake. Alaska was a show-off when it came to nature. For this early evening in autumn, the sky was awash in lavender with deep pink streaks, the colors shimmering on the waters of the clear lake. I let out a shout because I couldn't help it, my voice echoing back to me.

Impulsively, I tossed off my shirt, kicked off my boots, and shimmied down to nothing. I knew the lake would be bracingly cold, but I was ready. I needed this.

On the heels of a deep breath, I sprinted to the end of the dock and dove. My fingertips struck the cold water, and it enveloped my body in the next second. It was crisp and cold. My skin tingled every-where. With a single powerful kick, I surfaced, laughing at the shock of it and feeling more alive than I had in years.

Although I was freezing, I needed to be in the water for a few more minutes, just because. I dove under the surface briefly, savoring the feel of the water sliding over my skin. I felt wild as if this moment brought me back to myself. I surfaced again and glanced up at the dock, letting out a yelp.

The man standing there eyed me. He looked kind of cranky. That said, I couldn't help but notice he was handsome. Actually, handsome didn't even do him justice. He had auburn hair that shimmered with glints of gold from the setting sun. Even from here, I could see his piercing green eyes. Inexplicably, he wore a suit. His broad, well-defined shoulders filled it out very nicely. There weren't many occasions to wear a suit in Alaska.

"Um, hi?" I opened with.

The man rested his hands on his hips, stepping to the edge of the dock. "What are you doing here?"

"Swimming," I stated the obvious. Unfortunately, I was getting uncomfortably cold. I treaded water rapidly.

"You're putting on a show," he returned, clearly annoyed.

"For who?"

His hands dropped from his hips, one arm swinging in an arc and gesturing toward the shoreline. I followed to where he pointed and noticed a group gathered, visible in the backyard of a nearby property.

"I didn't hear anything," I said. "And I need to get out of the water if you don't mind. Also, you're on my dock."

I started swimming toward it, metaphorically gathering my dignity. I was naked in a freezing lake in Alaska in front of a sexy hot guy in a suit. What the hell was happening?

I swam to the ladder. I didn't even have to look because I knew exactly where it was. I'd swum in this lake so much in my childhood. I curled my hands on the rungs and called up, "Could you please turn your back? Or better yet, just walk away?"

When I heard footsteps moving away, I climbed up the ladder swiftly. The air was warmer than the water, but my skin prickled with goosebumps. I peered over the edge of the dock to see the man's back facing me.

I scurried onto the dock, fetching my clothes quickly while praying he was polite enough to keep his back turned the entire time. As soon as I had my jeans and shirt on, I announced, "All I have left to put on is my boots."

He turned around then while I sat down to lace them. A moment later, I stood as he waited in silence. "You can go now," I said.

"I figured I should make sure you weren't hypothermic before I left," he offered dryly.

Lifting my arms out, I spun in a circle. "I'm fine. What is going on over there, by the way? That used to be Bea Adams's place."

"Still is. She's my grandmother. She's getting married this evening."

My hand flew to my chest in surprise. "I didn't see anyone when I came out."

For the first time, his eyes held a glint of humor and his mouth kicked up at one corner. My belly did a little swoop. "We walked out onto the lawn just in time for your dive," he explained.

My cheeks got hot. Hell, I got hot all over. Which, all things considered, was convenient because I was still chilly from my skinny-dip in the glacial lake.

"Isn't Bea around eighty or so now?"

He nodded. "She still believes in love."

My lips curled into a smile. "Of course, she does. Please tell her I'm sorry for, I guess, naked diving in front of the group." I rolled my eyes, mostly to myself. "Give her my best wishes, please. I'm Alice, Alice Hall. You are?"

"Jonah. Adams," he added his last name almost as an afterthought.

"Nice to meet you, Jonah," I replied before stepping closer and holding a hand out. "I'm sure maybe we met if you ever visited when you were younger."

He nodded. "Maybe." His grip was warm, his hand engulfing mine. The feel of the calloused surface of his palm spun into the heat he'd elicited simply from half-smiling.

"What are you doing here?" he asked as he dropped my hand.

I took a quick breath. "I grew up here in Willow Brook. I live right there." I gestured to my childhood home, which was adjacent to his grandmother's property. "I just moved back to town. I'm taking over the veterinary clinic. What are you doing here?"

"Attending my grandmother's wedding."

"Oh, so you're just visiting?"

He shook his head. "I'm here for the wedding, but I'm a hotshot firefighter. I took a job on one of the crews in Willow Brook."

"Oh. Well, nice to meet you. Are you staying with Bea?"

He chuckled, the sound gravelly and sending heat scattering over the surface of my skin. This man got to me.

"I love her, but no. I don't need to live with the honeymooners. I'm staying in—"

"The place she used to rent out," I interjected.

Jonah nodded. "Exactly."

"So we're neighbors then."

Another nod. "I'm sure I'll see you around."

"I'm sorry for interrupting the wedding."

"Oh, Gram won't mind. Someone thought perhaps we should check who this was because Gram didn't think anyone was staying here."

"Let her know I'm back." I paused, twisting my lips to the side. "I hope I gave the wedding a story."

His eyes held a hint of a smile again, and my belly swooped. "You did. I'll be going then."

He turned and walked away, lifting a hand and waving over his shoulder.

Chapter Two

JONAH

As I stepped off the dock, I couldn't help but glance over my shoulder. Alice stood there, and even from a distance, our eyes collided. Electricity sizzled through the air. I forced myself to turn away. Stuffing my hands in my pockets, I continued walking, my stride long and even. My first glimpse of my new neighbor, and she'd been naked. My heart was still an echoing drumroll. All of my nerve endings felt electrified.

I hadn't felt this alive in years. To be specific, in four years.

Shaking those thoughts away, I hurried through the trees in my suit, which felt totally out of place in Alaska. Gram wanted a formal wedding, and I would do just about anything for her, so here I was in my suit.

A moment later, the trees opened up to the small field visible from the lake and offered a clear line of sight down to the dock. Alice was still on the end of the dock, but she had turned away and was looking out over the lake. The view was a stunner with the clear glacial water shimmering in the early evening and the mountains rising tall in the distance.

"You didn't have to chase her out of the water," Gram called over as I approached the group.

"I didn't chase her out. The water must be freezing. She said she was getting out because it was cold," I explained, feeling heat crawl up my neck and cheeks. I wasn't prone to blushing. What the hell?

My grandmother cast a dimpled smile at me as I stopped beside her. "I think it was a perfect start to my wedding."

"Yeah?" I prompted.

"It makes the day special and funny." She smiled over at her husband-to-be, Dennis. They were both old, weathered, wrinkled, and head over heels in love.

My father cast an indulgent smile at his mother before glancing down at my mother as his shoulders shook with laughter. She squeezed his hand where her fingers were laced with his.

I didn't like thinking about it, but Gram wasn't long for this world. She had a resurgence of lung cancer and was choosing not to get it treated this time. She'd smoked most of her life and had only quit a few years ago. The cancer had spread, and the doctor gave her maybe six months.

My chest felt tight, and I took a quick breath. "Well, I'm glad you enjoyed it."

Dennis chuckled.

"It's Alice, right?" someone asked.

I glanced over. "It's Alice Hall. She said she just moved back."

Gram's hand slapped her chest. "Aw, Alice. She's a sweet girl."

I nodded. My one exchange with her had been an exercise in restraint on my part as I tried to get my rampaging lust under control. It was blue from a distance, but the lake's water was nearly crystal clear up close. So, although the view of her body was blurry, it had been visible. My view of her diving in had been far too clear.

"I'll have to go over and see her. You should've invited her over," Gram scolded.

"She sent her best wishes," I offered.

"We'll see her soon enough." My grandmother glanced around. "Now where is our pastor?"

Just then, Janet James came out of the back of the house, waving. "I'm here!"

"Perfect," Gram said, clasping her hands together.

"Is Janet actually a pastor?" I asked.

"She's an officiant," my grandmother replied. She smiled up at me. "For the purposes of today, she is."

I knew Janet from the coffee shop she ran in town. She was also a dear friend of my grandmother's. Apparently, my grandmother had babysat Janet when she was younger, but now they both considered themselves old. Janet was a good twenty years younger than my grandmother, but I suppose the decades felt shorter as you got older.

Janet stopped beside me, slipping her hand through my elbow and squeezing. "Hi, Jonah. You're the best man, right?"

"Course he is. My friends are dead," Dennis offered laconically.

I couldn't help the laugh that slipped out. "Is that why I'm the best man?"

He grinned. "Most of my friends *are* dead, but I love you like a son. If you were an asshole, I wouldn't care if you were Bea's grandson. You definitely wouldn't be my best man."

I chuckled again. We swung into the wedding, and

it was over in a blink. The next thing I knew, we were enjoying the reception in my grandmother's house. She came over at one point, interrupting a conversation between my mother and me. My mother grinned and wandered off for more cake.

Gram nudged me in the side with her elbow as she looked up at me. "I think you should go get Alice."

"What?"

"She's there all alone. Her parents are gone."

"Gone?" I asked.

"Well, they died," she clarified. "She can visit with everybody. We've got all this food, and you and she can be friends. You should be. Your place is closer to hers than my house."

"I don't know where her house is," I hedged.

My grandmother blinked up at me. "Walk outside the front door and follow the path behind your house. It goes through some trees, and then there's her house. It's where she grew up."

"Is it okay for me to show up unannounced like that?"

"Tell her I sent you," she said with a firm nod.

Because it was my grandmother and I loved her, I couldn't refuse her. Of course, I was also curious about Alice. More curious than I wanted to be.

A few minutes later, I walked through the trees as instructed. I could see the roof of the small house where I lived as I passed it. Another moment later, the trees opened up again, and there was another house. It was single-story structure ranch style home with a bright-red steel roof.

A tall stand of birch trees was nearby with yellow leaves fluttering in the crisp early autumn air. I approached the house, wondering whether to go to the front door or the door on the side. Since the path led directly to the side, I walked up the stairs onto the side deck and knocked.

An unfamiliar sense of anticipation slipped through me, and I forced myself to take a slow breath. I was accustomed to feeling numb to just about everything. Even as a hotshot firefighter, an adrenaline-fueled job, I rarely felt nervous.

With her naked dive off the dock, this woman had brought something to life inside me. It felt like I was lumbering to my feet emotionally after a long hibernation.

The door swung open, and Alice looked up at me. I didn't know how long we stared at each other, but the entire moment felt electrified. She had silvery-gray eyes. They were wide with lush, dark lashes. Her dark hair, though damp and slicked back earlier, was drying in curls around her shoulders. A spray of freckles covered her cheeks, and her skin was flushed pink.

My body tightened. It felt as if sparks shimmered in the air around us.

"Hi," she finally said.

I had to clear my throat. "Hey. Gram sent me over here. She wants to invite you to the reception."

Alice blinked before a slow smile stretched across her face. "Of course. That's the kind of thing Bea would do. She probably mentioned that my parents are gone, and I'm over here all alone."

"She *did* say that, almost exactly," I offered.

"I'll come over. Give me a minute." Alice wore a tank top with a flannel shirt unbuttoned over it, paired with leggings. "I'll be right back."

My eyes lingered on the curve of her hips as she walked away. *Fuck me.* Alice gave off this earthy vibe and was delectably sexy.

A few moments later, we walked back along the

same path that had brought me here. Alice had swapped out her flannel shirt for a silky blouse over her tank top and slipped on a pair of cowboy boots. The only way to quell my body's fiery reaction to her was to avoid looking at her. I focused on the walk, dodging rocks and stepping over exposed roots along the worn path.

"So how is your grandmother?" Alice asked when she glanced sideways.

Our eyes locked, and yet again, it felt as if sparks shimmered in the air briefly.

"Good. I think."

"You think?" she asked.

I had just met Alice, but I knew she was important to my grandmother. It was open news around town that Gram was sick. As I pondered how to reply, Alice added, "Something's wrong."

We stopped, and I turned to face her. "Since you just got back, you obviously haven't heard. She's sick. Lung cancer. Although, I suppose it's everywhere cancer now. This would be her chance for another round of chemo, and she's decided against it." I tried to keep my tone gentle because I wasn't sure how much my grandmother meant to Alice.

Alice's stunning gray eyes widened as she drew in a quick breath. She pressed her palm to her chest. "Oh, wow. I'm so sorry."

I had adjusted to the news on an intellectual level. Still, this corner of my heart experienced a stinging burn every time I let myself think about it. Just now, the pain from that corner swelled, and my entire chest hurt. I took in a deep breath, savoring the crisp air carrying hints of spruce and the ocean not too far away. A raven called nearby with a magpie chattering noisily in return.

"She's really open about it. Since you asked, I thought I should be honest. As it is, she'll probably just blurt it out when she sees you. Everyone around town who knows her is aware."

Alice's lips curled into a small smile. "Of course. She always tells everybody everything."

That drew a dry chuckle from me. She smiled back. "I'm sorry."

"I'm sorry too. You grew up next door to her," I commented.

"She babysat me a lot," Alice stated with a small nod.

When she looked back at me, I could see the questions swirling in her eyes. "I grew up in Vancouver, British Columbia. My mother's family is from there. I have dual citizenship," I said, not sure why I provided that detail.

She nodded, her pretty eyes searching mine. "Thank you for telling me about Bea. Are you okay?"

"As well as could be expected, but not great. Knowing she may not be here much longer makes me wish I had more time with her before now." For a split second, it felt as if a door opened in my heart and mind, a door I preferred to keep closed. All of a sudden, a cacophony of emotions pummeled me. Emotions I wanted to ignore. They weren't about my grandmother, but with her being sick and facing her death with such grace and equanimity, it served to remind me of all I was trying to forget.

Alice stayed quiet as she nodded. I idly noticed when the wind caught her curls, blowing them lightly around her shoulders. "Are you ready?" she asked.

"As I'll ever be."

It didn't feel strange that we smiled at each other. At that moment, I felt a sense of kinship flaring between us. Alice understood my grandmother in a way only Gram's closest friends did. Gram would not want us to dwell, so we wouldn't.

A few moments later, we walked into my grandmother's house. As soon as Alice entered the room, Janet approached with a beaming smile. "Well, there you are, dear." She pulled her into a big hug, smiling over at me as she added, "I'm so glad Jonah fetched you."

Alice stepped back, laughing slightly. "He fetched me? I'm pretty sure he was ordered to get me."

Janet grinned, reaching over to squeeze my shoulder. "He is a dutiful and loving grandson, so of course, he went to get you."

I watched as Alice was pulled into the conversation with my grandmother, Dennis, Janet, and others, all of whom were glad to see her. Gram was thrilled to have the skinny-dipper show up at the reception. Alice shrugged off her teasing about it.

Meanwhile, I told myself the less I saw of Alice, the better. She opened doors inside me that were best left closed.

ALICE

As I drove down Main Street, I couldn't keep the smile from teasing my lips. Willow Brook, Alaska—home, sweet home.

The town was still small, although it had grown some since I'd left for college. The main street had more shops and restaurants and more cars. With it being autumn, tourist season was still in full swing with the last gasp of them here for any number of wildlife viewings and wilderness activities. When the sign for Firehouse Café came into view, my smile widened.

I turned my little SUV into the parking area and came to a stop. When I climbed out, I heard a voice calling, "Alice!"

As I glanced around, my eyes landed on Amelia, an old friend. "Hey!" I walked toward her.

Amelia was tall, leggy, and gorgeous with amber hair and eyes to match. She smiled down at me. "Good to see you!"

We hugged. When she stepped back, she added, "I was wondering when you'd get here."

"You were?" I teased.

Amelia was a few years older than me, and our parents were good friends when we were growing up. My heart stung with the burn of grief. My parents died in a boating accident. They'd been out fishing in the ocean, just for fun. A storm had kicked up, and their small boat had been swamped by the waves. I would never stop missing them, yet there was a sliver of solace in knowing they'd died doing something they loved.

"I heard you're taking over at the vet clinic. My mom helps manage it, so I have the scoop," Amelia said with a wry smile. "They also can't wait for you. The clinic has been using visiting veterinarians for over a year."

I chuckled. "Ah, that's right."

"Are you getting coffee?" she asked, gesturing toward the café.

"Of course."

She slipped her hand through my elbow. "Well, then let's sit together."

"Will you get me up to speed on all the gossip?" I teased as the bell jingled on the door when we walked in.

For a moment, I was flooded with memories. I'd worked at the Firehouse Café in high school. It smelled the same—rich coffee and fresh baked goods with a savory sweet scent lingering in the air. There was a low hum of conversation, and the small round tables scattered about the space were mostly filled. This old firehouse had been remade into the café— years before I could even remember it being an actual fire station. The old concrete floor of the garage where we stood now had been stained, and the fire pole was decorated with painted flowers. Brightly colored artwork hung on the walls, and the garage bay doors had been turned into windows, offering a view of Main Street and the mountains in the distance.

When my gaze reached the counter and I saw Janet chatting with a customer, tears stung at the backs of my eyes. I looked away quickly, colliding with Amelia's gaze. I saw the understanding in her eyes. "Feels the same, huh?" she asked softly.

I blinked away my tears and nodded. "It does. It's good to be home."

Our serendipitous encounter in the parking lot was exactly what I needed today. I knew I had always wanted to come home, but I'd also experienced trepidation every time I tried to plan it. I hadn't run away from Alaska. I'd gone to college and on to one of the best veterinary programs in the country in North Carolina. I had loved it. Then my parents died. The rush to come home for more than the funeral or a visit had this giant boulder in the path. Coming home meant facing how truly gone they were.

I had fretted and spun my wheels with a good job at a veterinary clinic affiliated with my graduate program. When I got a call from Amelia's mother, nudging me about the vet clinic and needing someone to take over, I had taken it as a sign from the universe. I'd needed some kind of impetus to push me along the way.

A moment later, we were standing in line. Amelia squeezed my elbow before releasing it.

"So back to the gossip," she offered with a grin. I looked over at her expectantly. "There's no way I can catch you up on all the gossip in one coffee visit."

Janet's voice reached us. "Girls, you're up."

"Oh!" Amelia took one step with her long legs and stopped at the counter.

I needed two steps to catch up.

Janet smiled at us. "So glad you're back, Alice," she offered. She flipped her braid off her shoulder. "I'd offer you a job, but I understand you're taking over at the vet clinic," she said, waggling her eyebrows.

"I am. I start next Monday. It's Wednesday." I hadn't been counting the days or anything.

"That gives you four days. You're coming to card night Friday," Amelia announced.

"That'll definitely be the quickest way to catch up on all the gossip," Janet offered with a sage nod. "I know what Amelia wants, but I don't know your coffee choice. Back in high school, your mom wouldn't let you have it."

I laughed softly. "I know. It was kind of ridiculous."

Janet shrugged. "It's neither here nor there. Do you like coffee now, or tea, or cocoa?"

"I like all of them. For now, definitely dark coffee and not sweet. Just a little bit of cream."

"Anything to eat?" Janet asked as she began prepping our coffees.

"I need a box of muffins," Amelia said. "We have a whole crew up on a project today."

"Oh, that's right. You have your construction business," I said, looking over at her. "Do you run the entire crew?"

Janet snorted. Amelia grinned at her and shrugged. "No, it's just me and my friend Lucy. Remember Lucy from high school? She moved here right at the end. She was a few years ahead of you."

"Blond hair, tiny?" I prompted as I sifted through my memories.

"Exactly. Total tomboy and a badass and married to Levi Phillips now."

"Levi the flirt?"

Janet snorted again. "He's still a flirt. He flirts with everyone and everything. But he's deeply in love. He's a really good man and a good father."

"I always liked Levi," I offered. "I was too young for him to flirt with me in high school. Anyway, if it's just you and Lucy, do you need a whole box of muffins?" I pressed on.

"We've got an electrician team there today, along with the paint crew. They're consulting with the couple whose house it will be." Amelia shook her head. "Men, they're all men."

"You know Amelia married Cade, right?" Janet asked as she passed our coffees over.

"I knew that. I heard you had a baby too."

"Oh yeah, she's one year old now. I don't know if you're ever going to have kids, but wow, it's a lot of work. Make sure you have people who can help," she said so earnestly I almost started laughing. "Seriously. My mom is worth her weight in gold when it comes to babysitting, and she freaking loves it, so you already have a built-in babysitter if you have kids."

I couldn't imagine dating or contemplating romance, much less considering the concept of babies. But I wasn't about to get into all that with Amelia.

I fished in my purse for my wallet, pulled out some cash, and said to Amelia, "I'll get yours."

"But I'm buying a box of muffins," she protested.

I shrugged. "Consider it my happy-to-see-you gift."

Amelia grinned. "I'll return the favor next time we run into each other here."

Just then, the bell jingled again, and I reflexively glanced over to see Jonah Adams walking in. The mere sight of him was a fiery jolt to my system.

Amelia followed my gaze. "Hey, Jonah," she said when he stopped beside us.

He dipped his head in acknowledgment. "Hey."

When he looked at me, I felt ridiculously nervous. "Hi," I said, my voice cracking on that single syllable.

"Good morning," Janet said.

Jonah's lips curled into a full smile when he glanced at Janet. "Good morning."

"What can I get for you?" she asked.

"Coffee." He slipped his phone out of his pocket, tapping the screen. "I'm picking up for the station."

Janet held her hand out with a grin. "Just show me the list."

Jonah's low chuckle sent sizzling tingles radiating to every corner of my body. Sweet hell. The effect this man had on me made no sense.

Jonah handed his phone over, and Amelia commented, "Delivery guy today?" At his nod, she added, "You should charge tips."

He flashed a wry grin. "I would, but plenty of us do coffee runs. Comes around goes around."

Amelia glanced back and forth between us. "You two are neighbors, right?"

Janet called over from where she was prepping coffees, "They are. They met after we all watched Alice skinny-dipping in the lake at his grandmother's wedding."

Heat flashed into my cheeks, and I rolled my eyes as I glanced at Amelia and cast a sheepish smile. "I didn't know anybody was there."

"Everyone was walking onto the lawn just when she finished stripping and dove in," Janet offered in clarification.

As if that detail made it less embarrassing. I shrugged.

Amelia grinned. "Perfect way to welcome yourself

home. Do you want to sit with us?" she asked, turning her attention to Jonah.

He shook his head. "Nah. Thanks, though. I need to hustle once Janet gets these coffees ready."

"Give Cade a kiss for me when you get back to the station," Amelia teased as she slipped her hand through my elbow again, lifting her coffee cup off the counter with her other one.

"I'll pass on that," Jonah replied. "I'm sure I'll see you both around."

We sat down at a table in the corner by the windows. I looked out over Main Street, commenting to Amelia when I looked back at her, "It still looks the same, but there's more."

"I know. I don't think Willow Brook will ever be huge, but we've grown a little."

"So Jonah must work with Cade since they're both hotshots?" I prompted, immediately cursing myself for letting my curiosity get the best of me. I was dying to know more about Jonah.

Amelia nodded. "Yep, that's how I met him. Cade is the superintendent for one of the crews there."

"How many crews are there?"

"Three hotshot crews and one town crew. They stay busy."

"Do you mind that?" I asked, genuinely curious.

"Mind Cade being a hotshot firefighter?"

I nodded. "Yeah. It's high risk, and he must travel a lot."

She cocked her head to the side, eyeing me thoughtfully. "I don't because he loves it. Of course, I worry when he's traveling, but he only travels during fire season. About half the year he's here. My job is dangerous too," she added with a shrug.

"How is your business going?"

"Busy," she said. "Need a side job?"

I shook my head as I laughed. "I'll be busy with the vet clinic."

"Are you running the whole thing?" she asked.

"I'll be the veterinarian, but that's it. Your mom's the one who called me about it. Do you know why Dr. Dan didn't try to sell the business?"

She pressed her lips together, her brow furrowing in concern as she replied, "He has dementia. Natalie, his wife, said he refused to sell. She told my mom she'd rather have someone he trusted simply take it over. I guess that's you."

"Oh," I said slowly. "Your mom didn't mention he had dementia."

"She said it's the gentle kind. He's really forgetful. He knows who I am, but he thinks I'm still in college," Amelia offered with a shrug. "I just go with it."

"Natalie hasn't mentioned anything about the plans for the clinic."

"I believe she wants to give it to you."

I stared at Amelia, my mouth dropping open before I snapped it shut. "Give it to me? I thought I was taking the job to be the veterinarian."

"That and the whole clinic."

I shook my head, my curls swinging with the motion. "Wow."

"Don't panic. Just talk to them. I'm sure you can figure something out that works for everyone."

Amelia glanced toward the door of the café as Jonah departed. Her eyes took on a gleam when she looked back at me. "Do you know who couldn't keep his eyes off you?"

"Uh, no?"

"Jonah." She waggled her eyebrows, and I felt my cheeks getting hot again.

"I doubt that," I said dryly.

"I don't," she said succinctly. "It was impossible not to notice."

I rolled my eyes. "I'm not looking for love."

"Are you seeing anyone?" she asked.

At twenty-eight years old, I was at that age where people often expected me to be paired up with someone. I took a breath, letting it out as I shook my head. "Life's been busy. It's not really a priority. Now that I'm here, I'll be busy getting started with the clinic, and I've got a few things to take care of on the house."

"Do you need help?"

I smiled. "I'm sure you're busy with your regular business, but thank you for asking. It's nothing major. With my parents gone, the house needs some catch-up on maintenance."

"You're a friend, and you're like family. Just say the word if you need help. Lucy and I can come out on the weekend and help out."

My throat felt tight, and tears stung my eyes. It was good to be home.

A short while later after we had finished our coffees and walked out to the parking area, Amelia said, "Give me your number. I'll text you for card night. I'm sure everyone would love to see you, and you can meet a few new people."

We exchanged numbers, and I left. As I drove by Willow Brook Fire & Rescue, I remembered Jonah staring down at me when I was naked in the lake. The mere memory of it sent a sizzle of electricity through my body.

Chapter Four

JONAH

One week later

I let my palms rest against the tiled wall, my head hanging forward as the steaming hot water pounded between my shoulder blades. I was beat.

We'd just gotten back from dealing with a late-season fire a few hours north. Like much of the western United States and Canada, Alaska was dealing with frequent fires. With one fire after another, it felt like a game of whack-a-mole sometimes to just keep things under control. We still weren't sure what started this fire, but the best guess was campers not following guidelines. After being gone for a week, we were all worn out.

I was beyond grateful that the fire station had kick-ass water pressure. The tension bundled between my shoulder blades started to ease from the heat. We carried heavy gear and worked our asses off in the backcountry. It didn't matter how fit you were. A full week of that pushed a body to its limit.

I straightened, letting my hands fall as I grabbed the bar of soap and quickly soaped myself. After rinsing, I toweled off and stepped out of the showers into the locker room area. I had just pulled my shirt on a few minutes later when Graham asked, "Battle scars?"

Graham Holden was the superintendent of our crew and a damn good one at that. He was level-headed but supportive. Being a hotshot firefighter took some nerve and plenty of confidence. There was a strain of men and women who did it who could be cocky and arrogant. Graham's crew had none of that. As far as I could tell, the other crews in Willow Brook didn't either. It set a tone, one I liked.

As much as I trusted Graham and felt comfortable, questions about the scars on my side elicited instant tension. It had been four full years, and I still contemplated flat-out lying whenever it came up. But that created another wrinkle of tension, and there was enough already.

I took a breath, letting it out quickly. "Before I became a hotshot firefighter, I was a teacher. There was a school shooting."

That was all I said. I had rehearsed those words many times. Graham was quiet as he studied me for a long moment.

"Oh hell. I'm sorry," he finally said.

I nodded. "Hell is one way to put it."

I sat down on the bench, pausing to pull my boots on.

"I think about that more than I wish I did," Graham commented.

I lifted my eyes to his as I tied my boots. "Don't blame you."

Graham had a teenage daughter who attended high

school. I wasn't about to give him the stats on the frequency of school shootings.

"Schools should be the safest places for our kids," I said, stating the obvious. I was a hunter. By no means was I anti-gun. But I knew from personal experience that we were in a dangerous place these days regarding school shootings.

"Sometimes it seems like guns matter more than our children's lives," Graham said somberly.

I straightened, resting my palms on my knees. "I know."

"You okay?" he asked.

That was a loaded fucking question. "I'm here," I replied. "I'm okay. It hasn't been easy. It's the reason I made a career change."

"Hotshot firefighting isn't exactly a safe career choice," Graham replied laconically.

I lifted a shoulder in a small shrug. "Maybe not, but the risks are more manageable. I couldn't go back after that." When the shooting happened, I'd just finished my graduate studies, and all I had left was to defend my dissertation. My plan had been to teach at the high school level for a few more years before looking for a university position. I could see questions swirling in Graham's gaze, so I prompted, "Go ahead and ask."

"Did anybody die?"

I felt a burning pain in my heart, pain that was usually cold. "Four kids and the shooter. A guidance counselor and the assistant principal. It was four years ago in Seattle."

He nodded slowly, his brow furrowed. "Honestly, I can't keep track. There are so many. Some stand out, but with others, I lose the details." He leaned back against the lockers behind the bench where he was seated across from me and let out a ragged sigh.

"No shit. I can't keep track either."

He looked at me quietly for another moment before offering, "I'm sorry. For what it's worth, I'm glad you're with us. You're fucking rock solid out in the field."

"I can handle a crisis. I'm good under pressure."

———

I'm good under pressure.

My words to Graham echoed in my thoughts that night. I *was* good under pressure. Except for the one time that really counted, I wasn't good enough. I took two bullets in the side. They went clean through and didn't hit a single organ, but the scars were bad. Semi-automatic bullets did that. The doctor said I was lucky as hell. I knocked the shooter down and saved a few more kids from getting shot. But it was too late for the four kids who were dead. I'd been dating the guidance counselor at the time. I didn't even know she was already dead when those bullets hit me.

The shooter came through the front entrance after arriving late for school. Tina's office was off to the side of the reception area where kids checked in when they were late. The shooter, a seventeen-year-old boy, had opened fire. She'd gotten shot four times in the side and once in her heart. The bullets came through the wall. They said she died quickly.

I had no visual picture of that, but my memory replayed the sight of the kids who died in front of me. There was blood smeared on the floor in the hallway. I would never forget the girl, shy with a quirky sense of humor, who died running straight toward the shooter as if she meant to knock him over. The shooter's brother had been shot at home before the student even came to school.

I still couldn't speak the shooter's name aloud when I spoke about that day. His name was Bill, a very common, almost ubiquitous name in the United States, a country of guys named Bill and guns. After I'd knocked him down, he'd bolted down another hallway and shot himself when he encountered two police officers. As with so many similar shootings, no one had to answer for it.

I shook my head, lifting the bottle of beer from the table in the kitchen and draining it. I was sitting by the windows, watching the lake. It was that twilight time. The sun had just slipped behind the mountains, leaving lavender fading to purple, blue fading to indigo, and streaks of gold fading into silver as the moon and the stars claimed the sky.

My grandmother had said it would be healing for me to come here when she told me about this job. She was right. Something about the beauty of Alaska that grounded one. Motion caught my eye, and I glanced over toward the dock, Alice's dock.

Moonlight shimmered on the water's surface, and I watched the silhouette of a person—Alice—walk down the dock. She stopped at the end. In a moment, she lifted her arm in an arc, her shirt dropping to the dock. From here, it was too far for me to see much of anything other than her silhouette. She stripped and dove into what I knew to be icy-cold water. I felt my lips curling in a smile. My hands twitched. I wanted to stand and walk through the trees down to the path that would lead me to that very dock and dive into the water with her.

But that was fucking crazy.

Chapter Five

ALICE

The next day

Hoarfrost covered the landscape the following morning, sparkling as the rays of the sun angled over it. I leaned my elbows on the windowsill and looked out, feeling a smile tug at the corners of my mouth. I loved autumn in Alaska. The change here could feel swift with the endless summer days shortening rapidly. The evergreens stayed green while the cottonwood and birch turned yellow and gold, their leaves fluttering in the wind. The fireweed had faded. The undergrowth on the ground was bright with color—reds, pinks, purples, and copper covering the landscape.

The lake hadn't frozen yet, but it would soon. Willow Brook had a larger lake, but this small one was fed directly from a glacier in the mountains. It had a blue glow to it. Simply looking at it, I felt a sweet twinge in my heart at the feeling of coming home.

The sun rising above the mountains in the distance

struck sparks on the lake's surface, the water glinting like diamonds in the crisp air. Motion caught my eye, and I glanced to the side to see a man appearing out of the trees.

Jonah.

Just thinking his name and my belly swooped, tingles radiating throughout my body. I watched as he walked down to the shoreline. He walked to the end of the dock. My breath caught as I watched him strip down quickly and efficiently. Unlike me, he didn't get naked. He had on a pair of fitted boxer briefs. From here, I could see his muscled shoulders and the clean lines of his back as he raised his arms above his head and dove into the water. I breathed in sharply, knowing the sensation he was feeling, almost viscerally experiencing it myself from a distance. Icy-cold water enveloped you, shocking your system to life and invigorating you in a way nothing else could.

His head broke through the surface, and he leaned back, looking up at the sky. I wondered what he saw. Rather, I wondered what he was looking for.

I told myself to look away, but he might as well have been a magnet for my eyes. I watched as he dove under again and swam quickly back and forth, almost as if he was swimming a set course of laps. After a few minutes, he climbed back on the dock, dried himself with a towel, and walked back up the hill, barefoot and all but naked

I had to fan myself, and my heart was racing by the time he disappeared into the trees. Almost embarrassed, I turned away from the window as if he'd seen me watching. I laughed softly to myself as I crossed over and drained the last of my coffee. I filled the mug again with what was left before quickly rinsing the coffee pot and filter, putting them away for tomorrow morning. Or this evening, when I couldn't sleep and drank coffee as if that would make the situation better.

After a few swallows, I set the mug down and rested my hands on my hips, circling the kitchen. I needed to make this house different. It ricocheted with the memories of my childhood and, of course, my parents who were gone.

My mind replayed that image of Jonah walking up the hill, his muscled chest visible from my kitchen windows.

You do not need to be thinking about a man, my mind pointed out.

No shit, I volleyed back.

I had been so stupid after my parents died. I fell into what I thought was a harmless flirtation with one of the owners' sons at the vet clinic where I worked. He was cute and chatted with me about our shared love of all animals.

Up until my parents died, I had been a focused, practical woman, finishing up my vet degree, getting my hours to be independently licensed, and working my ass off at my job. I dated here and there but never had much time for it. After my parents died, I'd become a ball of emotional need.

I'd been careless and not noticed what an ass the guy was. All was well until he began blackmailing me to give him prescription meds. Some medications were used for humans and animals. This guy wanted the anxiety meds and some pain meds. He had photos of me changing from the locker room at the clinic.

All of his kindness became an obvious manipulation. I'd refused to give him the medications. I still don't know what I would've done if this job hadn't come up when it did.

"Dumb, dumb, dumb," I muttered to myself. I still felt foolish beyond belief.

The one time I was vulnerable, I'd ended up in a bad spot and still worried about what he might do with those photos. "I should've reported him to someone other than HR," I said to myself in the room.

"Should've reported who?"

I let out a squeal and spun around, my hand flying to my chest. Jonah stood in the kitchen doorway, fully clothed. His hair was damp.

"Uh, I didn't hear you knock."

He shook his head. "Your door was wide open. I saw it from the side." He thumbed over his shoulder toward his house.

"Oh," I managed.

He reached for the doorknob, turning it, glancing my way, and offering, "It seems a little loose."

My heartbeat was starting to slow from being startled. "It is. I haven't fixed it. When it's locked, it stays shut, but..." My words trailed off as I shrugged.

He reached into his pocket and pulled out one of those multi-use tools.

"Do you always carry that?" I asked as I approached.

He glanced over at me, his eyes glinting with his smile. "Yes, actually. It's handy. Hang on, I can fix it right now."

I watched as he quickly tightened a few screws, tested it, and then adjusted it again. He stepped back, saying, "Try it."

I walked over and closed the door. It closed snuggly. I smiled over at him. "Thank you."

He dipped his chin in acknowledgment. "No problem. By the way, I don't normally show up unannounced, but your door was open, and I wasn't sure if you were here."

"No, I appreciate it. If I notice your door open, or anything open, I'll stop by too. You never know what might walk in. We don't have too many bears, but they're around. There are also lots of rabbits, porcupines, and squirrels."

When he smiled again, my belly shimmied, and my breath became short in my chest. I stood there smiling at him, feeling foolish the moment I realized that was all I was doing. I cleared my throat. "We should exchange numbers. That way, we can call or text if anything comes up. Since we're neighbors," I offered, willing the heat rising in my cheeks to dissipate.

In another moment, he texted me his number and I replied to confirm.

"Thank you for checking on me," I commented.

He opened the now-fixed door, stepping back outside. Belatedly, I added, "And thank you for fixing my doorknob."

He turned, dipping his chin quickly. "You're welcome. I'm sure I'll see you around."

I watched as he walked down the steps and along the slate walkway onto the grass and then disappeared into the trees between my house and his. We really weren't that far apart, at best maybe a quarter mile. Just close enough for me to watch him as he walked all the way to his house, glancing back just as he opened the door.

Heat flashed into my cheeks. I was still standing in the doorway, where he could see me. Flustered, I closed the door, pressing my back to it and taking a deep, shuddering breath.

Jonah Adams, my new neighbor, made me stupid and foolish. I resolved to get that under control.

Chapter Six

ALICE

I held the keys in my hand as I stood at the back door to the veterinarian clinic. I'd been here with my parents when we used to take our family cat and dog for annual checkups. The most memorable visit had been when our dog had gotten too close to a porcupine and ended up with a nose full of porcupine quills. She'd been distraught and whining.

I slid the key into the lock, almost surprised when it worked. It's not that I thought I had the wrong keys. It's just that I couldn't believe I was going to run this clinic. I was accustomed to being a small fish in a big pond at my last job. That clinic had been huge, with twenty veterinarians working there. For now, this place would just be me.

"I'm here," I whispered as I walked into the back hallway.

Natalie, Dr. Dan's wife, was meeting me here in half an hour. I had decided to come a little early so I could look around.

I closed and locked the door behind me. I stopped at the end of the hall, glancing to the side to see a row of light switches. I turned them all on. The hallway lights came on, and two of the office lights blinked on.

Anticipation fluttered inside. I stood there for a minute as a smile stretched across my face.

"Wow," I whispered to myself.

I slipped the keys into my purse and peered into one doorway to see what must be a supply room. Office supplies occupied shelves against the wall. I stepped in and ran my finger along the shelf, surprised to discover there wasn't any dust. Someone must have cleaned.

Shelves lined all four walls with the office supplies to one side. The rest of the shelving had clinic supplies. I saw bandages and other things with containers neatly labeled.

I walked out of that room and crossed the hallway into another room to see more supplies and an empty refrigerated storage space. Leaving that room, I walked down the hallway. There were two examination rooms for pets and a surgery room. There was a break room with a circular table and a counter with a microwave, a small refrigerator, and a coffee pot. I smiled as I looked around before a dash of alarm struck me. I needed staff. I could handle cats and dogs and horses and more, but I needed help with the rest.

"Breathe," I whispered to myself as I stepped out of the break area and went through a doorway that led to the front.

The front area had a circular desk with phones and a computer. The monitor was old, one of the big bulky ones. There was even a credit card swipe machine. I had so many things to contemplate.

I scanned the waiting area. Chairs lined the walls, and photographs of pets decorated the space, along with a bulletin board with thank-you cards and photos pinned on it. I sat down at the reception desk, wondering what to do now. I had a list of questions. My eyes landed on a notepad beside the phone. I slid it over and snagged a pen from the small mug filled with writing utensils.

Receptionist?

Vet tech?

Office supplies?

Billing?

When Amelia's mother, Georgia, had called me about the job, she had explained I'd be taking over as the veterinarian. I hadn't been prepared to take on the whole thing.

Motion drew my eye to the front door. Georgia was there, along with Natalie. They waved as Natalie slid a key into the lock, opening the door and walking in together.

Georgia smiled widely. "Come out here for a hug."

I left my purse on the desk and stood, walking out to the waiting area. Georgia was like an aunt to me as she was one of my mother's best friends. She had babysat me many times over the years when I was little.

She still smelled the same, a comforting, fresh powdery scent. She hugged me tightly and then stepped back, gesturing to Natalie. "You know Natalie, right?"

"Of course. You were the receptionist here."

Natalie smiled as she pulled me into a quick hug. "I was. What do you think?" she asked as she stepped back and gestured around the space.

"Everything looks great, and it seems like someone cleaned."

"That would be me, dear." She grinned, her eyes twinkling. "Now, we need to plan."

"We do," I said, nervousness tightening in my chest. "When I took the job, I guess I didn't realize how much I might need to do. I'm realizing I need staff, billing, and everything lined up. I feel foolish because I didn't think this through," I said honestly.

"We've got you covered," Georgia said. "It hasn't been closed. We've had temps covering the clinic a few weeks of every month. Natalie knows all the billing stuff and will show you what was set up before. I used to help with ordering supplies and things. We were thinking of giving it a month or two. We'll get you up and running, and you can decide if you want to modernize things. There's a waiting list."

"A waiting list?" I squeaked.

Natalie nodded. "Honey, there's no veterinarian nearby except for Anchorage. We can have you filled up with patients inside of a month."

I took a breath, trying and failing to quell my nerves. "But I don't even have any income to pay you two."

Natalie shrugged, way more mellow than me about this. "There's a surplus."

"I'm sorry, what?"

"Look, I know this is a lot. We wanted you to get here and hopefully stay. Dan would like you to have the clinic. He remembers your parents and you. We don't need the money from selling it. We're all set retirement-wise. We'd rather it go to someone local who we care about. The accounts have enough money in them now to pay staff for a few months. You don't need to pay Georgia and me, but we'll find someone to help with the front. Once you're up and running, you can hire a vet tech."

I stared at her. "Oh," was all I could say.

Natalie smiled. "It will be fine. It's a fairly simple business."

Georgia studied me. "When Natalie asked about you, I thought you'd be perfect. In a way, I'm doing this for your parents. Making sure you're home and on your feet."

My throat felt tight, but all I could do was nod.

Natalie was all business. "I'll help get all the accounts and things transferred to you. We just needed you to be here to sign everything. What do you say? We'll take the week to get everything up and running on the backend, then start scheduling for you."

I gave my head a shake, trying to absorb everything. "Um, okay," I squeaked. "Are you sure about this?"

"Absolutely. We've been making it work with temps, but I finally decided we had to have a plan."

"*You* are the plan," Georgia interjected with a firm nod.

"Wow," I finally said. "Well, I guess, let's get going."

I was ready. Or I told myself I would be. I had left my job behind and moved back home. I really had no choice but to dive in and make this work.

Chapter Seven

JONAH

A few days later

I had settled into a rhythm at my house, but I didn't realize how much it would affect me to have Alice next door. I kept telling myself it was ridiculous. Hell, I had my nosy grandmother on the other side. Nosy as she was, she also left me to my own devices. And, of course, I didn't think about her the way I thought about Alice.

One of my habits was to stop by to check in with my grandmother every few days. After work one day, I walked through the trees to her place, knocking lightly on the door and calling, "Gram!"

I heard giggling and then someone shushing someone else. I laughed to myself, just about to turn away when the door opened. My grandmother was there, and her cheeks were pink.

"Hi, sweetie," she said.

My grandmother was the only person who'd ever called me sweetie.

I smiled down at her. "Oh, I thought maybe you were busy."

"I was, but I'm not now. Come in."

"No need. I just wanted to check in and see how you were doing."

"I want you to come in," she insisted as she swung her door open wider and stepped back.

I wasn't going to argue that point with her, so I walked into the kitchen, glancing up to see Dennis seated at the counter.

He smiled over at me. "Good to see you, Jonah."

"You too, Dennis."

My grandmother closed the door behind me and walked over to the counter, lifting something wrapped in foil. "Here, this is for you." She handed it over to me.

"What is it?"

"My brownies with a caramel swirl," she said, leaning forward as she spoke in a conspiratorial tone.

"Oh, wow," I replied. "I haven't had these in years."

"I know. Seeing Alice reminded me I haven't made them in a while. She used to love them when she was a little girl. Just like you loved them."

"She made two batches," Dennis said. "I told her there was no way I wasn't gonna have any."

I chuckled as I grinned over at him. "That's a must. Well, thank you." I turned my attention back to my grandmother.

"You can go now." She walked back over to the door and opened it.

I smiled down at her. "You didn't have to let me in," I added.

She shrugged. "I wanted you to have these. Now you do."

A short while later, I was in my kitchen thinking I

should heat those brownies. I put them in the oven on low heat. I was actually a little hungry and should've thought to grab some takeout or swing by the grocery store. I lifted my phone to make a note in my calendar to remember to go to the store tomorrow after work. I lived and died by my calendar.

As I set my phone back down, I happened to glance up and look out toward the lake. Alice was walking down the dock with a basket held in her hand. I watched her reach the end and sit down. I wasn't sure what she was doing, but I was curious.

Impulsively, I lifted my phone and texted her.

Me: *It looks like you're having a picnic on the dock. I have dessert.*

A moment later, my phone vibrated with her reply.

Alice: *I am having a picnic. I have enough for two. If you bring dessert, I'll share.*

Maybe it was stupid, but I didn't really care. I grabbed the warm brownies out of the oven, snagging a kitchen towel to wrap around them to help retain the heat. Moments later, I walked through the trees and down the hill to the dock, a sense of anticipation humming inside.

I didn't want to contemplate the way Alice made me feel more alive than I'd felt in years. Even when I was firefighting in risky situations, everything felt muted. This was helpful in a crisis because I could keep my focus where it needed to be. Until Alice, I hadn't realized a part of me missed feeling something, feeling anything. Yet the mere existence of her broke through that fog and numbness. In turn, it amplified my emotions. Because I was afraid, afraid to let anyone matter too much.

It's just dinner, I told myself as I felt the soles of my feet with each step walking along the dock.

Alice was sitting cross-legged and smiled as she glanced over her shoulder, calling, "Hey there!"

"Hey, yourself," I called in return.

My pulse sped, thundering hoofbeats inside my chest as I stopped beside her. She'd spread out a blanket and had a bottle of wine with a tray of cheeses and meats, crackers, and a small bowl with some kind of dip. The scent of fresh bread wafted to me.

"That smells good," I commented as I lowered myself to the blanket and stretched out my legs.

"What's that?" she asked as I set the brownies on the blanket beside me.

"Gram's brownies with caramel. I thought I'd keep them wrapped in a towel because they're warm. I put them in the oven a few minutes ago."

"Oh yum," she breathed. "I've had her caramel brownies before. They're amazing."

I chuckled. "I know."

We smiled at each other for a moment. I didn't know what to do with the feeling of—the only word I could put to it was intimacy—between us. We'd just met a mere week and a half ago. And maybe the first time I saw her, she was bare-ass naked, but that wasn't it. There was a sense of comfort when I was around her. That in and of itself was unsettling for me.

She swung her hand in an arc over the blanket. "I have charcuterie, dip, and freshly baked bread."

"You made all this?"

"Well, I didn't make the cheese and the meats for the charcuterie, but I did make the pretty arrangement." She moved her hand over the platter with a flourish, glancing up at me with a grin.

"Looks very good," I offered

"I also made the bread. It's just a loaf of basic white bread, my favorite. It's nice and soft. I have an olive oil drizzle with basil and red pepper, and an arti-choke cheese dip."

"Nice," I murmured.

"I needed something to eat. My parents and I used to come down to the dock and do stuff like this. I thought I would celebrate my first week at the vet clinic. I hope you like red wine. I have beer up at the house if you prefer."

I shook my head. "We don't need to walk back up. I have beer at my house too. I'll take some wine."

She glanced into the picnic basket, offering, "I even have cups. I didn't know you were going to text me, but this little basket still had all the picnic stuff from when my parents were around."

"I'm sorry they're not here," I offered.

She gave me a polite smile. "Thank you."

She made it easy for that topic to simply drop by pulling out a paper plate and handing it to me. "I'd get it all ready for you, but I don't know what you like."

She lifted another plate from the small stack.

"I'm pretty easy when it comes to food."

I waited for her to start serving herself, but she looked over and gestured. "You first."

A few minutes later, I looked out over the lake. With it being autumn, the air was crisp with a bite to it. The sun was setting as the stars became visible in the twilight sky.

Glancing at Alice, I said, "This is an amazing place to grow up."

She finished chewing a piece of cheese and nodded. "Absolutely. It's a bounty of beauty. When I tell people about it who aren't from here, sometimes I think they think I'm exaggerating."

I finished off a slice of bread. We fell into another comfortable silence, and I discovered yet one more detail about Alice. She was easy to be with, and silence didn't feel pressured with her. That was another sharp edge for me. I wasn't accustomed to feeling at ease. I hadn't since the shooting.

I was too bitter, too cynical, and way too realistic about what the world had to offer to let myself allow anyone to matter too much.

Aren't you cocky? my mind taunted me. I volleyed back with a silent, dry chuckle.

I didn't know what this thing with Alice was, but I knew if it went anywhere, I couldn't keep it superficial. I didn't know how I knew that when I barely knew her, not really, but I did. I knew on a visceral level, on a heart level.

"Do you need more wine?" Alice's voice was throaty and melodic.

Even that sent a sizzle through my system. Hell, every detail about Alice affected me.

I glanced down at my almost empty cup of wine and shook my head when I met her gaze again. My eyes landed on the picnic basket. "That's a well-stocked picnic basket, by the way."

She smiled, a wistful look entering her gaze. "Like I said, it was my parents' basket. I guess it's mine now. They used to hike a lot, and we came down here for evening picnics often when the weather was nice enough." Her eyes shifted out toward the lake.

"It's a beautiful place for a picnic."

When her silvery-gray gaze met mine again, my entire system felt jolted, as if lightning sizzled through the air between us.

"It is." She cocked her head to the side, studying me quietly. "Your grandmother lives here, but you didn't grow up here," she pointed out.

"Are you sure about that?" I countered.

She rolled her eyes. "Of course, I'm sure about it. I won't pretend I know everyone in town, but if you grew up here, I would know it. Your grandmother lives next door." She gestured in the direction of my grandmother's house.

"Fair enough," I replied with a chuckle. "My father was born here, but he went away for college. My mother is from British Columbia. I think of the Pacific Northwest in general as kind of a suburb of Alaska."

Alice had just taken the last swallow of her wine and sputtered on it, reaching for a napkin. After she dabbed at her mouth, she shook her head slowly. "You're kind of right. Geographically speaking, most people would think that was crazy. But if you live in Alaska, you know you can't really fly here, at least not in the US, without going through Portland or Seattle."

"What do your parents do?"

"My father's a marine biologist, still is. He took a job at a university in Seattle. My mother was a teacher and was teaching until just a few years ago."

"Seattle is in a pretty area. Where were you in the city?"

"We lived in a small town on the outskirts. We came up to Alaska in the summers."

She looked thoughtful, offering, "I think I remember you coming up. How old are you?"

"Thirty-four. You?"

"Thirty. Back then, four years felt like forever."

"It is like forever," I agreed.

"Did you move up here for the firefighter job?"

Chapter Eight

JONAH

I nodded. "Yes," I said simply, leaving out so many details behind that decision. It was a chasm of information to avoid, but I did. I wasn't about to get into all that with Alice. As much as possible, I avoided talking about the school shooting. I had wanted to eventually take a university job, like my father. I still had that undefended dissertation hanging out there. Instead, I got shot, watched four kids die, and learned a woman I had been dating had also died. The idea of walking into a classroom of any kind left me in a cold sweat.

Blessedly oblivious to my train of thought, Alice gestured toward my empty plate. "Brownie?"

"Yes. Do you think they're still warm?" I asked as I reached for the towel-wrapped brownies.

"I bet they are."

When I unwrapped them and felt the warmth, I grinned at her. "Success." I carefully opened the foil to find what had to be a full tray of brownies tightly lined up in rows. "I can't remember the last time I had Gram's brownies."

"For me, it would've been the last time I came home to see my parents," she offered.

When our eyes met, I saw pain flickering there for a moment, but it disappeared quickly. She looked down, carefully lifting two brownies and putting them on my plate.

"How do you know I want two?" I teased.

"Because I want two and probably more," she quipped with a wink.

I bit in and the rich chocolate and warm caramel flavors broke across my tongue. I closed my eyes as I let out a moan. After I finished chewing, I opened them to see Alice's own eyes were closed as she savored the flavor.

"Fucking amazing," she said flatly after she swallowed and opened her eyes.

"Definitely."

We each ended up eating four. Alice carefully wrapped the remaining brownies. "I bet those will be gone in another day."

"Do you want some?" I asked.

She looked up at me, starting to shake her head before I added, "You know she'll make me more."

A smile curled the corners of her mouth, and my pulse pounded in response as if clapping. "Excellent point. Let's walk up to my place. We can put them in a container. They'll just rattle around loose in this picnic basket."

I helped Alice clean up, which mostly consisted of me watching as I handed her items to tuck into the basket. Moments later, we walked up the hill together, angling toward her place. I followed her into the kitchen, and she set the picnic basket on the corner of the counter.

"Give me a sec. I'll get a container. Are you sure

you don't want them all?"

She looked up at me, and for a moment, I couldn't remember what she was talking about. The gears in my mind clicked into place, and I nodded. "Of course. Gram will be thrilled to know I shared her brownies with you."

Alice grinned. "Well, by all means then." Her gaze sobered. "I'm really sorry she's sick."

I took a quick breath. "Thank you. I am too. Right now, I'm sort of in denial. I know it intellectually, but I'm hoping she'll last longer than they think."

"There's nothing wrong with a little denial. They always say it's good to live in the moment. At this moment, she's here, so let's celebrate that."

"With dark chocolate caramel brownies," I added dryly as she turned away to fetch a container out of a cabinet.

"I'm with you there," she replied, her voice laced with subtle laughter.

She took half the brownies because I insisted. The sound of the lid snapping closed on the container was loud in the quiet kitchen. Alice looked up at me. "Thank you for the brownies and for joining me for dinner."

I didn't realize I was standing so close to her and wasn't even sure how I ended up there. Her kitchen wasn't that large. The door that came in through the side was behind me, and there was a counter along the wall where the door was and another that faced the lake. Although it was dark, I knew where the lake was. To another side was a little breakfast nook nestled into a bay window.

I forced myself to focus. "I think I should thank you. You're the one who fed me." My voice had a raspy edge to it.

Her hand was resting on the container. She lifted her other hand, catching one of her curls and spinning it around her forefinger. Her curls were an unholy temptation, dark and a little wild and untamed. I wanted to bury my hands in them and kiss her.

Apparently, my body was ahead of my brain. Because, in another second, I had reached over, catching the curl and letting it slide through my fingers. Her eyes widened slightly, and I heard a little hitch of her breath in her throat. As I looked down at her, I noticed the spray of freckles scattered on her cheeks.

Because I was all in on being reckless at this moment, the next thing I knew, I brushed my knuckles lightly across her cheek, murmuring, "I love your freckles."

She looked up at me, her big silvery-gray eyes blinking. Desire curled around us like wisps of smoke, the very air humming with the vibration of our need.

"Jonah—" she began.

"Shh," I murmured.

I wasn't even sure if that was for her or me. My need to kiss her was trampling over any remaining sanity. I knew if I thought at all, I would stop myself.

Alice's eyes searched mine as I waited. My only rational impulse was to give her just enough time to stop me, but she didn't.

She placed her palm on my chest, startling me when she leaned forward and pressed a kiss at the base of my throat. My pulse leaped under the place where she touched me. Her lips were soft and warm and sent licks of fire chasing over my skin. She drew away slightly, peering up and offering, "It's the perfect spot for a kiss."

Her fingertip traced a circle around it before feathering along the edge of my collarbone. What little restraint I had snapped loose. I took another step and slid my arm around her waist, murmuring, "Now would be the time to tell me this is stupid."

"Well, I hope kissing me isn't stupid," she teased as she leaned up, sliding her hand around the back of my neck and flexing into me.

Our lips met, and what started as a brushing touch, teasing and testing galloped out of my control rapidly. I hadn't kissed a woman in years. Oh, I hadn't been chaste all this time. But kissing was intimate, and intimacy was something to be avoided at all costs.

I supposed kissing was like riding a bicycle. Maybe it had been a while, but I slipped right into it. Alice arched up against me, her curves soft and warm. She let out this little gasp into my mouth, and my tongue swept out, laying claim to her mouth. She didn't hesitate, not even for a second. Her tongue glided sensually against mine. Our kiss turned deep, searching, and wild just as there was a sharp knock on her kitchen door.

We broke apart, staring at each other, our breath heaving. I was startled by the depth of my response to her.

I gave my head a sharp shake, asking, "Are you expecting company?"

She looked a little dazed when she shook her head. She straightened her shoulders and stepped back. I instantly missed the feel of her softness, her warmth, and how very alive she felt in my arms.

She walked past me, opening the door. "Oh! Hi, Bea."

"Alice, have you—" My grandmother's eyes landed on me. "Well, there you are!" she exclaimed as she stepped into the kitchen.

Alice closed the door behind her, casting an amused glance at my grandmother and then me.

"Are you looking for me?" I asked.

"Of course, I'm looking for you. There are no lights on at your house, and you always leave your lights on."

"I do?"

Gram shrugged, waving a hand airily. "You do. You're weird about it."

"What's weird about leaving the lights on?" Alice interjected.

My grandmother shrugged. "I don't know. I was just coming over to see if you happened to have seen Jonah. You have because he's right here in your kitchen," she pointed out.

Gram's eyes narrowed as she looked back and forth between us, and I sensed that she picked up on the bonfire flickering between us. I hoped she didn't get pushy.

"I was just bringing Alice some of your brownies," I said quickly.

Gram beamed at me and then Alice. "Oh, you are such a good boy!" She stepped to my side, sliding her arm around my waist and squeezing tightly.

I hugged her closer, dropping a kiss on her cheek before she stepped away. "For you, yes. I thought maybe Alice would like some. I think you gave me a whole tray. You just wrapped it in foil, so it didn't seem like so much," I teased.

"Of course, I gave you a whole tray," she clucked. "I'll make them every week. Now that Alice is back, I'll make extra," Gram said, rubbing her hands together.

Chapter Nine

ALICE

I waved goodbye as Bea and Jonah left. After a moment, I caught myself watching for too long. My eyes greedily lingered on Jonah's broad shoulders.

I quickly shut the door, leaning my back against it and taking a deep breath.

What the hell am I doing?

Better yet, what the hell are you doing kissing Jonah?

My critical mind wanted to know. It was a rather obvious question, all things considered.

I had no idea and *definitely* no good answer. I didn't need to lust after my neighbor whose grandmother was dying, whom he obviously adored and doted on. I took a breath and let it out, pushing away from the door.

Crossing over to the kitchen windows, I looked out over the lake. I'd gone and kissed Jonah. I let out a ragged sigh. Why did he have to be so handsome and sexy?

I had important things to do, things to focus on, and none of them involved getting tangled up with my hot new neighbor.

———

The following morning at the vet clinic, I went through a long list that Natalie had typed up for me. She'd even written a sample job description for the job she did. Good Lord. I had a lot on my plate.

I quickly copied and pasted the job description she wrote and put it up on the town's local online job board. I doubted I needed to use one of the big job websites, although I supposed I could do that if I didn't get any good responses.

I prayed I got some good applicants. I was going to lean heavily on Georgia's and Natalie's insider knowledge of Willow Brook and its current residents. I hadn't lived here since high school, and it was safe to say my high school social knowledge was not particularly useful at this point.

After that, I got to work reviewing the supplies. Georgia assured me she and Natalie had stayed on top of things for the temps they had had in the clinic. But we all had preferences, and I wanted to make sure we had the things I needed and preferred.

When the vet clinic number rang, I glanced at the phone mounted on the wall, eyeing it suspiciously before I was galvanized to hurry over and answer it. We were in business, and I needed to schedule appointments if anyone called.

"Hello, Willow Brook Veterinary Clinic," I said, feeling a surge of anticipation inside as I spoke the name of my new business aloud.

"Hi, Alice."

The fizzy anticipation faded instantly and cold dread balled in my stomach, anxiety spinning rapidly in my chest.

Shit, shit, shit, I hissed silently in my brain.

I took a quick breath. "Hi, Tyler."

"I heard you had a new setup going on," he replied.

"Tyler, please leave me alone."

"It's not that simple, Alice," Tyler Black replied.

Tyler Black, otherwise known as the fucking gaslighting asshole who was still trying to blackmail me even though I had nothing to give.

"I can't help you," I said flatly.

"Sure, you can," he returned smoothly. "You have a new vet clinic."

"No."

"Alice—" he began, his tone laced with warning.

I was so fucking done with this guy. "Tyler, don't call here again. If you do, I will report you to the police."

"Oh, really? I still have those photos."

Nausea welled inside, but I forced myself to stay firm. "I will. You can't intimidate me anymore."

I hung up the phone, taking a shaky breath as I walked in a tight circle in the supply room.

I still couldn't believe the clinic had done nothing, *nothing* when I told HR about his med theft and the camera he'd set up in the women's locker room there. I didn't understand why he kept targeting me. He had to know I couldn't help. There was no way I'd let myself get blackmailed into supplying him with meds at my new clinic. If I did that, it would never end. I was already in over my head here. If I didn't own the home I inherited from my parents, I would be so fucking screwed. As it was, I was praying that I would start bringing in money in time to pay the utilities.

I shook my head, resolving to check the number he'd called from and block it from here. If only I could count on Tyler facing actual consequences.

Chapter Ten

JONAH

Several days later

I had resolutely avoided the urge to go down to the dock when I saw Alice there for the past two evenings. Ever since the night we kissed and had been conveniently, or inconveniently, interrupted by my grandmother, I'd told myself this irrational lust for Alice would pass.

It didn't change the fact that my eyes were drawn toward her house every morning when I left for work. I could see it through the trees. The days were getting shorter, and her kitchen light was on in the mornings now. I shouldn't have been so curious about her, but I was. I savored, knowing she was up early.

I climbed into my truck and drove into town, tapping my dashboard screen to answer a call when I recognized my parents' number.

"Hey, Mom."

"Jonah! How are you this morning?"

"I'm fine, Mom. I'm headed in for work. How are you?"

"Doing well. You haven't called in over a week," she said.

My mother was a worrier. She always had been. Her worrying about me had multiplied exponentially after the shooting.

"I've just been busy, Mom. Are you and Dad coming up anytime soon?"

The unspoken in my question related to my grandmother's illness. They hadn't visited since her wedding.

"That's why I was calling. We're going to come up next weekend. I think perhaps we'll come up and stay for a bit. How do you feel about that?"

"I think that'd be great. You know Gram would love it."

"We'll talk to her about it. Meanwhile, how are you?" she repeated.

I bit back a sigh. "Mom, I told you I'm fine." I brushed away the subtle irritation that rose inside.

My parents didn't love my career choice after the shooting. My father had been more accepting of it, but I felt like my mother was still trying to turn back time. I sensed she thought if I fell back in love with teaching, that meant I was okay. I *was* okay. Just not the kind of okay she wanted.

"You did," she said softly. "We can't wait to see you."

"I'll pick you up at the airport. Text me your flight times so I know when to come get you."

"Jonah, you don't have to do that," she insisted.

"I know I don't, but I want to."

"Okay then. Once I make the reservations, I'll text you the itinerary."

I turned onto Main Street, commenting, "I'm almost at the station, Mom. I need to go."

"Of course. I love you."

"Love you too, Mom."

I tapped my dashboard screen to end the call and took a breath, ignoring the tight feeling in my chest. Tangled up in the tragedy of that day four years ago was the fact that I felt like I was letting my parents down. I thought my father was glad I had moved to Alaska because he always wanted to come here when he retired. Yet I knew they both wanted something else for me. My mother had finally stopped pointing out that I couldn't be a hotshot firefighter as a lifetime career. *No shit*, I thought to myself.

Maybe I would go back into teaching someday. Yet anytime I thought about walking into a classroom, my stomach turned. Much as I told myself the likelihood of experiencing more than one school shooting was slim, they were still far more common than I ever wanted to contemplate.

When I saw the sign for Firehouse Café ahead, I made a quick decision to stop. I could use another cup of coffee and one of Janet's bagels.

A few moments later, I was waiting in line when I heard the bell jingle behind me. It wasn't the bell that drew my attention but rather the prickle of awareness that raced up my spine. Glancing back, I knew I was going to see Alice. And there she was. Her dark curls were damp. She was looking down as she put her keys in her purse. When she looked up, her eyes met mine, and it felt as if a flame traveled through the air between us.

"Oh, Jonah!" she exclaimed. She stopped behind me in the line.

My eyes lingered on the spray of freckles on her

cheeks and the subtle pink flush. "Good morning, Alice." It felt as if spurs dug into the flanks of my pulse, nudging it faster and faster.

"How are you?" she asked politely.

"Well, and yourself?"

"Uh, busy." She let out a low laugh with that.

"Just busy? Not good, bad, or somewhere in between?" I teased lightly.

"Too busy to think about it," she returned with a quick grin.

The door to the café opened again, and Holly Fox walked in. I knew Holly through her husband, Nate Fox, a pilot who sometimes ferried the crews to and from fires.

Holly stopped beside us, glancing from me to Alice, before saying, "Nice to see you, Alice. We can catch up as soon as you get a clue and move along." She gestured with her hand to the counter.

I glanced over my shoulder before casting a quick grin back at Holly. "Moving right along. Good to see you too, Holly."

"Oh! I wasn't paying attention," Alice replied, bouncing forward behind me when I stopped at the counter.

Janet smiled amongst the three of us. "Good morning, all. I think you were first. Jonah."

"I was, and I'll cover everyone's coffee," I offered.

"Wow. Well, I'm not gonna say no to that," Holly said.

"It's only fair. Apparently, we were holding up the line," I said dryly. "I'll take my usual and one of your egg extravaganza bagels." I glanced at Alice, then Holly. "Go ahead and order."

After they ordered, Holly asked, "Do I get food too?"

"I said I'd cover it," I returned.

Holly beamed. "Excellent. I'll get an egg extravaganza too. And, you know, you should bring some coffee to the station."

I chuckled and turned back to Janet. "You know what? Just make me one of the take-out trays of coffee. Get whatever Nate likes and a variety so I don't have other people giving me shit for not bringing some for everyone," I said wryly before rolling my eyes at Holly.

"I'm an opportunist," she said with a shrug. She glanced toward Alice as we collectively stepped to the side of the counter. "So, I hear you're taking over the vet clinic."

Alice nodded. "I am. Haven't seen you in years," she added.

As Janet began prepping our coffees and called our food order back to whoever was working in the kitchen, Holly announced, "I need to hug you."

She threw her arms around Alice, squeezing her tightly. Alice was smiling by the time she stepped away. "Good to see you, Holly."

"Same. This town needs a regular vet, so I'm glad you're taking over. Georgia and Natalie have been holding down the fort, and they've had temps, but we need someone who's here all the time. Our dog is fussy about the vet, so he needs someone he knows. I was thinking once you're ready to roll, we can schedule a meet and greet," Holly said earnestly.

Alice's lips stretched into a slow smile. "A meet and greet?"

Holly nodded enthusiastically. "We'll pay for it. He's a totally crazy thing at the vet even though he's usually sweet."

"Some animals are like that. I'll be happy to schedule an appointment."

"Excellent. Now tell me everything else."

"Everything else?" Alice prompted, her brows rising. "That's over ten years to cover. I'll condense it. I went to college and then to vet school. As you know, my parents passed away. I'm back, and I'll be taking over the vet clinic. That's it in a nutshell," she offered with a quick nod. "How about you?"

"Never left town, went to nursing school. I work at the hospital. I'm a nursing supervisor in the ER department there, and I married Nate."

"I heard. I think that makes sense."

"It does?" Holly pressed. "Because I'm not so sure about that sometimes. Just last night, he woke me up with his snoring."

I snorted. "You two are a good couple."

Holly shrugged and teased, "I just like to find small things to complain about. We were friends for years, and he's Alex's best friend, so..." She sighed. Alex was Holly's twin brother.

"I knew Nate and Alex were friends, but I didn't realize they were close before you two were married," I commented.

Holly smiled slightly when she glanced my way. "You're new in town. Well, sort of because you didn't go to school here even though your grandmother's here and your dad's from here."

"I think that's another way of saying I'm not fully up to speed on the historical gossip around town."

Alice nudged me lightly with her elbow, adding, "I'm way behind, so you don't need to feel left out."

Holly glanced between us. "I try to fly under the radar."

Janet handed over a to-go tray of coffee. I held them in one hand as I fished my wallet out with the other.

Janet glanced at Holly. "Easy for you to say when you are definitely one of my most reliable sources for gossip."

Holly shrugged, entirely unrepentant. "I am. I just don't want people gossiping about me. I take a control-the-information kind of approach."

Janet rolled her eyes as she grinned. Holly's gaze bounced from Alice to me before she commented, "Janet knows everything. If you didn't know this already, you want to keep her on your side."

Alice smiled at Janet, replying, "I already knew that. It's not hard to keep Janet on your side. She's a total softy."

"Jonah is always nice," Janet said firmly. "Now, out of the way. Your sandwiches should be ready soon, but more people are behind you."

We scooted over to the side of the counter to wait. We walked out together a few minutes later. Holly waved and drove off after exchanging numbers with Alice.

Alice looked up at me and lifted her coffee cup slightly. "Thank you. You didn't have to get my coffee."

"I wanted to."

"You already gave me your grandmother's brownies, and now this coffee. I feel like I owe you one."

"Did you forget you let me share your picnic the other night?"

Alice flushed slightly. "I didn't do much for that."

"There was fresh bread," I insisted.

She laughed softly. "True. I'll get you a coffee next time, or we can have an actual dinner."

"I'll take you up on either," I replied.

A moment passed as we simply stood there, looking at each other quietly, and it occurred to me that perhaps the time had stretched too long. Alice had that effect on me. I wanted to linger in her company. It wasn't as if we were doing anything special.

I cleared my throat. "I'll see you around. If you insist, you can get my coffee next time I run into you here."

Her eyes held mine, and my pulse raced. I had to force myself to step back, lifting my hand in a wave. "Catch you later."

She blinked before nodding. "Thanks again."

I watched as she climbed into her SUV and drove off before leaving.

Chapter Eleven

ALICE

Maisie glanced up with a smile. Amelia looked from her to me, offering, "Maisie usually wins."

"That's her I-won smile," Lucy interjected.

I couldn't help but laugh. "I see."

Maisie shrugged. "My father is basically a card shark. He was really into gambling, and he was actually good at cards. He also fucked my life up because of it, but the one thing I got out of it is I'm really good at cards. I don't like to cheat to lose, so I sit out sometimes."

"Because the rest of us are inferior with our skills," Madison chimed in from my side.

We were all together in Madison's kitchen for the card night Amelia had mentioned the first time I ran into her. It ended up being canceled that weekend, but she'd texted me yesterday about this one. Apparently, the group got together a few times a month when it worked out.

I knew Amelia well and had a passing acquaintance with Lucy from when she moved to town in high school. I also knew Holly, Ella, and Susannah. Madison was new to me. She had moved to town recently and was engaged to Graham Holden, who I also knew from high school. While I hadn't been in the same grade in school with everyone here, most of us had grown up together.

Paisley was also new to town. She was a firefighter and on the same crew as Jonah. I also knew Mae, who, like me, had moved back to Willow Brook more recently.

"Paisley wins sometimes," Maisie offered as she shuffled the cards and handed the deck to Amelia, who was sitting beside her. "I'm going to pass on this game."

"The least you could do is give the rest of us pointers when you sit out," Holly teased, nudging her lightly with her elbow.

"I don't care if I win or lose," I said as Amelia began dealing the cards after shuffling the deck again.

"Well, you might after Maisie wins every time," Madison commented with a grin.

"She's sitting out this time," I pointed out, gesturing toward her.

Maisie's eyes crinkled at the corners with her smile, and her brown curls swung slightly when her shoulders shook with laughter. "I just like to hang out with everybody."

"When did you move here?" I asked.

"Just over three years ago," Maisie replied.

"She works at the fire station. She's like the center of the universe there," Susannah interjected.

Maisie rolled her eyes. "I handle dispatch, and I'm the main receptionist there. If that qualifies as the center of the universe for the fire station, I guess I am," she teased.

"And Beck fell in love with her." Ella offered this with a solemn tone.

"I heard Beck was married and has kids. How many kids do you have?" I asked.

"They have two," Lucy chimed in. "I'm telling you, I have no idea how you handle two. One is more than enough for me."

Maisie shrugged. "Once you get through the baby phase, it's not so bad. It is a lot of work, though."

I glanced around the table, asking, "How many of you have kids?"

I promptly discovered I was way behind the times upon learning how many of my friends had children. After that update, I glanced amongst the group. "Well, I guess I'm late at this."

Amelia curled an arm around my shoulder, squeezing before returning her attention to her cards and organizing her hand.

"You're not behind," Susannah said. "Having kids is definitely not a have-to thing."

"So what *is* the deal?" Holly asked.

"The deal with what?" I prompted.

She pressed her lips together, narrowing her eyes. "I'm asking about whether you're with anyone or if having a baby is even on the radar for you."

"I'm not with anyone, and I haven't even thought about babies yet. Unless I wanted to do it all by myself, which I'm not sure I can handle."

Lucy snorted. "Anyone who can, blows me away. I bow down to all the single parents in the universe."

"It seems like you and Jonah are friendly," Holly commented next, her tone casual and airy.

I knew better because I knew Holly well. "He lives next door to me in his grandmother's extra cabin."

Holly nodded. "Mmm. I think he likes you."

Heat flashed into my cheeks, and I hoped it wasn't obvious. "Uh, I don't think so."

As soon as I said that, my mind replayed that kiss. Oh, that kiss! Why, oh why, did Jonah have to go and be so freaking good at kissing?

"For all I know, he's seeing someone," I added with a shrug.

Holly let out a sharp laugh.

"What's so funny?" I asked.

"That is a slick way to get information," she said.

Amelia glanced my way and then toward Holly. "Cut her some slack. Alice just got back to town a few weeks ago."

"Also, I need to schedule an appointment for our hamster," Lucy interjected.

"I'll be opening for appointments in two weeks. I'm looking for an assistant to help out front."

"We're getting back to Jonah in a second," Holly replied, "but you should ask Tiffany."

"Tiffany?"

"Tiffany Mills. She just moved back to town," Holly said.

"Oh, is she looking for work?"

"That's what she told me when I ran into her the other day," Amelia offered.

"Hang on, I'll text you her number," Holly said.

"I haven't talked to her in years," I replied. "We were friendly in high school, but it feels a little weird to cold call and ask her to work for me."

"I'll tell her about it. If it's okay with you, I'll give her your number," Holly suggested.

"That sounds good."

"Okay, back to Jonah. He's not dating anyone. I know that for a fact," Holly said.

"Is there anything you don't know?" I teased.

Several women laughed around the table as Holly shrugged unabashedly. "No. I just like to stay up to speed. Jonah definitely keeps to himself."

"Do you know why he moved here?" I heard myself asking before I could think better of it and keep my mouth shut.

Holly nodded. "Yeah. His grandmother. Has he told you the whole story?"

"I'm not sure what the whole story is. We haven't spent much time together. I saw Bea at the wedding after they saw me skinny-dipping."

"What?!" Susannah burst out with Madison casting me a wide-eyed look.

"I swear, it was an accident." I quickly explained what had happened.

"Way to come home and make an entrance," Maisie said.

"So what's the story on Jonah?" I pressed.

"It's really sad," Madison said from my side.

I looked at her. "What do you mean?"

She glanced around the table, explaining, "He told Graham."

"Told Graham what?" I asked.

"He used to be a teacher and was in a school shooting. Four kids died. He saved more by getting them out of a hallway, but he got shot. A woman he was dating also died. The shooter shot himself," she explained succinctly.

I gasped, pressing my palm to my chest. "Oh, that's terrible!"

"It's heartbreaking," Susannah added.

"He rarely talks about it," Madison offered. "Graham said he only learned about it because he asked him about the scars on his side when they were at the station changing one day. Graham figured it was some kind of injury from firefighting and then felt like an ass when he realized it wasn't."

Holly nodded. "His grandmother told me he was shot twice."

I thought about the shadows I'd seen in his eyes and the carefully guarded quality about him. "Wow," I whispered. "That's just tragic."

"Sometimes I don't even want to send my kids to school," Maisie said. "Yet we will, and we'll convince ourselves it's okay even though it's not."

"I can't imagine something like that happening here in Willow Brook," I said, glancing around the table.

Lucy placed a card on the table before replying, "I'm sure most people say that wherever it happens."

I drove home that night, and it was impossible not to wonder how Jonah was feeling after what he had been through. There were many things I didn't know about him. I barely knew him, but I knew his grandmother. I knew she loved him and that he was a good man. I couldn't imagine what it was like for him to carry the internal scars from what he witnessed and experienced.

After I parked in the gravel parking area near the road and walked through the trees to my house, I reflexively glanced at his place. I wanted to go over and hug him and tell him the world wasn't all bad. My pull to him was powerful. I told myself it wasn't because of that kiss. It couldn't be because of that intense attraction between us.

Chapter Twelve

JONAH

Graham lifted his hand in a wave as I glanced around the restaurant at Wildlands, a favorite local hangout connected to a travel resort for tourists. I aimed in his direction, weaving through the tables and pausing to say hello to a few people. I reached the table, nodding toward Graham, Russell, Chase, and Rowan.

"Hey, guys. How's it going?" I said as I snagged one of the empty chairs and sat down.

They had snagged a large round table in the back corner of the restaurant. Usually once a week or more, a group from the fire station would meet here. Graham, Russell, Rowan, and Chase were on the same crew as I was, although Cade and Beck, who arrived a moment after I sat down, were on a different crew.

"I'll tell you how it's going," Beck said as he sat beside me. "I'm fucking starving."

I grinned. "Well, good thing you're here."

"Let's get a bunch of appetizers," he replied.

"Works for me," I commented.

"We were at a training exercise all day, and

someone forgot to bring granola bars," Russell chimed in, casting a friendly glare at Graham.

Graham shrugged. "Dude, I'm not in charge of food. I'm just the crew superintendent."

A few minutes later, a server had stopped by the table, handed us beers, and assured us a collection of appetizers would be on the way shortly.

"So, what do you think of Willow Brook?" Beck asked after she departed.

In my time here at the station, I had learned Beck was the male version of the nosiest person in an office.

"I like it. It's not like I'd never been here before, though. I used to come up with my parents in the summer," I replied.

Beck dipped his chin in acknowledgment. "I remember. We used to go fishing sometimes. You planning to get a boat?"

"I have to decide if I want the one my grand-mother says she's giving me."

"If it's in decent shape, you should keep it," Cade offered from across the table.

"That's what I was thinking," I replied. "It's in storage, so I'm gonna swing by and look at it."

"Can you stay in that place on her property as long as you need to?" Russell asked.

I nodded. "I can. If you haven't heard, she's sick. She tells me she wants me to take her house. My parents are thinking of retiring here, so I think they'll probably stay at her house."

"Why not settle down and have kids? Then you'll need a bigger place," Russell offered.

I grinned over at him. "Dude, are you in a hurry or what?" I teased. "I'm not planning on settling down or having kids anytime soon."

Beck got a text from his wife, and blessedly, the

conversation moved away from me. Not that I had any secrets, but I preferred not to be the focus of attention. The smaller the circle of my personal life, the better.

A few hours later, I left, thinking I was glad my grandmother had told me about this job. It was good to be near her in Alaska while she was sick. I also really liked the crew and the other guys at the station. Everybody was solid and down to earth. It was such a huge change of pace from the life I had led before I came up here. I hoped the reset I was looking for would hold.

A short while later as I walked toward my house, my eyes were drawn over to Alice's house. We actually parked in the same area, a small gravel pad with a shared path that diverged, one leading to hers and the other to my place. My pull to her was almost magnetic. The urge to find some random excuse to swing by was strong. But I kept telling myself that the kiss had been stupid and a fluke. I needed to keep my distance.

The following morning, I walked along the path to the parking area. The air was brisk with my breath misting in the air. Everything was covered in frost. With the sun just cresting over the mountains and its rays angling across the landscape, there was a glittering path where the warmth melted the frost. I stopped for a moment, glancing toward the lake through the trees.

Gram had insisted Alaska would be healing. She had said, *"That kind of natural beauty offers something nothing else can give you. It calls to your heart."*

Her words echoed in my thoughts, and I took a deep breath, letting it out. The process was slow, but my heart was healing stitch by stitch.

"Good morning."

I turned to see Alice approaching from her branch of the pathway. I felt my lips tugging into a smile. "Good morning," I returned, waiting for her.

She stopped beside me, turning to look out over the lake. "Can't beat waking up to this," she commented, her voice low.

"No, you can't," I agreed. "I still marvel at it every day. Does it ever get old?"

My gaze shifted to Alice—her slightly damp curls, her silvery-gray eyes, the fresh quality she conveyed. The spray of freckles on her cheeks was endearing. I didn't think I'd ever noticed anyone's freckles. Her cheeks were pink from the cool autumn air.

Her curls swung when she shook her head. "It doesn't."

"Do you think it's because you were away and came back?"

Her lips curled into a slow smile as she shook her head again. "I was born here." Her arm swung in an arc from the trees to the lake. She turned toward the mountain range where the sun was rising before her arm fell to her side. "I never got tired of it, and I missed it the whole time I was away."

When she looked back up at me, my heart started kicking hard against my ribs. That startling and intense attraction sizzled through the air. I thought I saw the answering flare in her eyes.

I wasn't thinking, but then, Alice had that effect on me. I stepped closer, lifting a hand and sliding it through her curls, smoothing them back from her cheek and palming it. I couldn't look away as she peered up at me. "What are you doing, Jonah?"

"This," I whispered in return, just before I dipped my head and brushed my lips over hers.

That subtle touch sent a fiery jolt through me,

startling me. I lifted my head, staring at her, trying to understand us.

Alice looked as stunned as I felt. "What—?" she began, just before a voice called, "Good morning!"

We broke apart, leaping back guiltily. The voice was unmistakable—my grandmother.

We turned together to see my grandmother appear on the path. I hoped she'd only had a view of my back. She would be way too excited to catch me kissing Alice.

"Good morning, Bea," Alice said as my grandmother approached and stopped beside us.

"Good morning, dear." She leaned up, pressing a kiss on Alice's cheek before turning to me.

I leaned down for her to reach me. She kissed my cheek as I curled an arm over her shoulders and squeezed gently before she stepped back.

Her sharp gaze bounced between Alice and me. "So, you're kissing now."

A wash of pink rose on Alice's cheeks, and I felt my own face heating.

Chapter Thirteen

ALICE

My cheeks burned, and I couldn't help but look at Jonah. His green eyes were bright, and his cheeks held a subtle flush. He smiled down at his grandmother, shrugging lightly.

Her eyes twinkled with a sly gleam as she glanced back and forth between us again, lacing her hands together and squeezing them. "Well then, I won't say anything else about it."

"Yes, you will," Jonah countered.

I cleared my throat, and he chuckled as she looked from me to him again. "Okay, fine, I probably will. For what it's worth, I think you're perfect for each other."

Jonah pressed his lips together, glancing at me and offering, "I'm sorry. I think you know she's nosy."

I took a breath, scrambling for any composure to be found, which wasn't much. I simply shrugged, replying, "I'm aware of that." My cheeks were still on fire.

Bea's gaze sobered. "I am nosy, and that's fine, but since I'm dying, I will grab a chance when I can."

Jonah looked utterly wrecked for a moment. My own heart felt pinched, painfully hard.

"Gram," he murmured.

She stepped up to him, sliding her arm around his waist and squeezing. "I'm just being honest."

"Do you have to point out that you're dying? Maybe the doctors are wrong," he protested.

"Maybe so. But my point still stands." With that, she stepped back, adding, "I have to go because I have a doctor's appointment."

"Do you need a ride?" Jonah asked.

She shook her head. "I can drive perfectly fine." She gave him a quick peck on the cheek before turning and climbing into her car.

We watched in silence as she started her car and drove away. I looked over at him, asking, "Are you okay?"

He ran a hand through his hair, letting it fall. When I saw the sadness and worry in his gaze, I wanted to hug him and tell him everything would be fine.

He took a breath, replying, "I guess I have to be. I love her."

"I know," I said softly. "She's not my grandmother, but I love her too. Lots of people love her."

"She's very lovable," he said with a wry smile. "Even if she *is* nosy as hell."

Heat flashed into my cheeks again, and I let out a little laugh. "She is."

"I'm sorry about that," he returned.

"No need to apologize. I can handle it."

We stared at each other for a moment before he said, "I have to go."

"Same here. I'm sure I'll see you soon, either here or in town," I offered.

"We're headed out to a fire. I may not see you for a week or so."

"Oh. Be safe!" I called as he climbed into his truck.

"Always."

———

"So what do you think?" I asked.

Tiffany smiled at me. "I'm in. This is totally up my alley."

"Are you sure?" I pressed.

This was my one and only interview for the job officially titled office assistant, but what was really the help-me-not-lose-my-mind-and-make-this-clinic-run job. As promised, Holly had contacted Tiffany about the job, and Tiffany had called me yesterday. I remembered her from before, but I hadn't spoken to her in the years since I'd left Willow Brook. Our social circles had overlapped, but we hadn't spent too much time together with her a year behind me in school growing up.

"I am totally sure." She brushed her dark hair back from her shoulders, her blue eyes bright and intent as she held my gaze.

I had to hold back the urge to throw my arms around her in relief. "Okay, well, we have a lot to do. This place has been running on fumes and temps. As far as I can tell, the office end of things is still in the land of paper. Natalie and Georgia have done a great job, and it's all organized, but I think there's a lot to do as far as updating."

"I am all about it. My goal will be for you to focus on the pets and for me to focus on the humans. I want to make it so you don't have to stress about all the stuff behind the scenes."

I took a deep breath, letting it out in a whoosh. "Oh my god. Thank you," I said fervently.

Tiffany smiled again. "You seem really worried. We've got this."

"Well, when Georgia told me about this, I think she purposely made it vague. I knew I'd be the only veterinarian here, but I wasn't completely clear that I'd literally be running the entire clinic. I'm a little over-whelmed."

Tiffany chuckled. "Maybe they were waiting to see if you'd go for it."

I shrugged. "Probably. So, uh, when can you start?"

"When do you need me to start?"

"Today," I said bluntly.

"I'm in."

"Seriously? You can literally start today?"

"Absolutely."

"Oh, wow. This is perfect. I need to have Natalie or Georgia come by. They have a whole contract and the pay and HR stuff to do. Your first step will be tran-sitioning us from the paper system they've been using to a computerized system for payroll and the pet charts. I've done a little research on the backend, and there are plenty of options. Otherwise, I need help sorting through the schedule so I can get started."

Tiffany rubbed her hands together. "I am ecstatic. We'll get your schedule filled up within a few weeks."

"I hope so. As far as I understand, Dr. Dan started phasing out two years ago. They've been having temps come in, but nothing consistent."

"Willow Brook may be a small town, but we desperately need a vet. We serve pretty much the whole surrounding area, except for Anchorage. I was talking to my dad about it when I told him I was going to come in and talk with you about the job. Chase was telling me that he's had to drive to Anchorage for his dog. Are you going to do emergencies?" she asked.

"During the daytime hours. They have a clinic in Anchorage that's always covered the evening calls. I think that's best because I'll never be able to breathe until I hire another vet. I'm nowhere near that point. Once I have enough business, I'll hire someone."

Tiffany rubbed her hands together again. "Let's call Georgia or Natalie, so I can start."

I loved her enthusiasm. I was almost on the verge of tears of relief when I smiled over at her. We stood, and I gave her a quick hug. "I know we haven't seen each other in years, but I'm so relieved it's you. I trust you. I know you can do this, and I just need some help."

"I'm thrilled. I need a job, and I love organizing people. This is perfect."

I quickly texted both Georgia and Natalie. Georgia said she'd be there in an hour. "Let's do a tour while we wait."

By the end of the day, I felt like I could breathe. Tiffany was on top of things. After the HR part was handled with Georgia, Tiffany set me up with a shared online calendar that we would use until she figured out the best system for appointments. She was already working on figuring out a small payroll system and an online portal for billing and clients.

She was at the reception desk in the front when I stopped in to check with her. I'd spent most of the day going through the supplies and organizing the pet charts.

She grinned up at me. "I already have half of your week booked. Next week is almost full."

"Holy shit. How did you do that?"

"Georgia showed me the list of people waiting to

schedule appointments for their pets, and I called them. We've got this. Speaking of pets, do you have one?"

I sighed. "Last year, my dog passed away. I knew I'd probably be moving, so I decided to wait. I think I'd like to look for a rescue. Do we still have the rescue program in town?"

Tiffany nodded. "Yup. I asked my dad because I just moved back. Lynnie Stuart still runs it. I already found the records because Dr. Dan used to do all of the spaying and neutering for them."

"Oh, of course! I should go down there and check with them."

"Let's go find your pet. Dog or cat?" she asked.

"Dog. I like cats, but I'll start with a dog and maybe get a cat for the house. I'd like to have a dog I can bring here."

"Let's go now," she suggested.

I hesitated for a second, but then I realized there was no reason not to go now. "Let's."

Chapter Fourteen

ALICE

I turned onto the main road that would lead us out of downtown toward the small animal rescue program that had been in Willow Brook for as long as I could remember.

"How long have you been back in town?" I asked as I glanced over at Tiffany.

"Not much longer than you. Only a month," she said with a grin.

"Are you glad to be here?"

She cocked her head to the side as I slowed along a turn in the road. "Yes. You know being from a small town in Alaska is its own thing. You think you want to get out and see the world, and you do. It's good to do, but I missed home like crazy."

"I know exactly what you mean," I agreed. "Where are you staying?"

"Holly hooked me up with her old apartment."

"Oh, nice! Where is it?"

"It's right in downtown Willow Brook. Where are you staying?"

My heart squeezed for a beat as I replied, "My parents' old house. Or I guess mine now."

"Oh, that's right." She pressed her palm to her chest. "I'm sorry about your parents."

"Thank you. It's been a few years, so I've adjusted. I miss them like crazy, but it's life, I suppose. I'm sorry about your mom," I added.

"Thanks," she said quietly.

"How's your dad?" I asked

"Oh, he's good. You know my dad."

I grinned over at her. "I do. He's always been such a nice guy."

"Always will be," she said lightly.

"Should I get the whole update? Like are you seeing anyone, all that?" I prompted, waving airily as I drove.

"Not too much to update. I'm single. That's probably for the best because relationships aren't my thing. Chase and his fiancée are expecting, so I'm super excited about that."

"Are you serious? Chase is having a baby?" Chase was her older brother.

"Well, he's not having it, but he's the father," she quipped. "His fiancée is Hallie Thomas. She lives in Anchorage, but she's moving here. He's a hotshot firefighter, so he's friends with Jonah. He's next door to you, right?"

"Oh, wow, you're up to speed on everything," I teased.

Tiffany chuckled. "I go to the Firehouse Café on the regular, so it's hard not to get caught up on local gossip."

I grinned. "Excellent point. So it's the next road, right?"

"I think so. I think there's a sign," she said, her words trailing off.

I slowed, and there was a small sign—Willow Brook Animal Rescue.

A few minutes later, Tiffany and I were waiting in the reception area, which had photographs on the walls of various pets and their new families and a desk with a sign. We had followed the instructions and rang the bell and were still waiting.

I slid my gaze to Tiffany after perusing the bulletin board, saying, "Do you think anybody's here?"

"Someone's here," a man's voice called.

Tiffany and I approached the desk, glancing at each other when no one appeared. Another moment later, a man came out of the door beside the desk. His alert gaze bounced from Tiffany to me and back again. He had dark blond hair and rich brown eyes. He moved with a rangy ease.

I felt like I recognized him, but I couldn't place him. Tiffany beat me to it when she said, "Wes Stuart?"

"Tiffany Mills?" he returned before he glanced at me. "Alice," he finally said, sounding more confident about that than Tiffany. My brain finally registered the memory. This version of Wes wasn't the Wes I recalled. He'd been brainy and quiet in high school, also a tad nerdy. Now, he was handsome and fit and gave off an outdoorsy vibe.

"Wow," Tiffany said. "I don't remember the last time I saw you."

Wes, otherwise known as Wesley, flashed a quick smile. I studied him for a moment, waiting for some kind of reaction. I'd found myself doing that with men ever since my kiss with Jonah. I wanted to think it was just my rusty libido, not Jonah. My libido had nothing to say about Wes.

"It's nice to see you," I said. "I just moved back recently."

Tiffany grinned as she looked from me to Wes. "Same here."

"Well, that's the theme then. I just got back last week. I'm taking a position as a hotshot firefighter." His gaze shifted to Tiffany. "I believe I'll be on the same crew as your brother, Chase."

Tiffany's cheeks were a little pink when she looked at him. "Oh wow. Small world."

Wes cast a wry smile. "Willow Brook *is* a small town."

"If you're going to be a firefighter, what are you doing here?" I asked.

"If you didn't know, my mom runs this place. It's her volunteer thing that she's done forever. I'm helping out."

"Well, that's great. I don't remember your mom because we were kids back then, but I'm taking over the vet clinic. Apparently, we have a contract with you all to handle vet care, spaying and neutering and so on."

Wes nodded. "Good to know. I'll let my mom know you're taking over at the clinic. She handles all the admin stuff. Are you here for one of the animals? As far as I know, everyone's healthy," he said, a wrinkle of worry forming between his brows.

"I'm here for a dog. I want to adopt one," I clarified.

"We have those," he quipped. "Do you want to come back and meet everybody?"

A few minutes later, we were standing in a room in the back area, and I was looking down at a three-legged mutt. She looked to be a mix of all kinds of dogs. Tiffany was sitting cross-legged on the floor as she scratched behind the dog's ears.

"Does she have a name?" I asked Wes.

He shrugged. "No. She just showed up last night. Somebody dropped her off while we were closed."

"Are you serious?" I squeaked.

He nodded. "Unfortunately, it happens."

"I know it happens, but Willow Brook is so small, and it's not safe to leave a pet out loose with moose and bears around. I can't believe someone would do that."

He murmured his assent, but his gaze had drifted to Tiffany. I sensed there was some kind of something between them. Tiffany stood, brushing her hands on her jeans, and he brought his attention back to me. "I just finished feeding her. We'd probably be calling you soon about a regular checkup."

"Do you have cameras here?" I asked.

"We do, but they tied her up near the mailbox on a tree just past the drive, so it was well out of view."

I approached the dog, sinking down on my knees and running my hands over her body, gently checking her out. She was a sweet girl. I carefully ran my hand over the upper joint of her missing leg. "At some point, she had surgery to remove her leg. I wonder if we have records at the clinic."

"Will it matter?" he asked.

"We have photos for every dog, so probably."

She was brown with blond highlights and a pretty little thing. Her ears hitched halfway up, and her eyes were soft and brown. "Hey there, honey," I murmured softly.

She nuzzled my chin and curled into me in response. After a few minutes of petting her, I glanced at Wes and Tiffany, who appeared to be in conversation. "She's the one," I said firmly.

"She's all yours," Wes said, looking away from Tiffany to me.

"Is there an adoption fee?" I asked.

"For you, no," he offered with a grin.

"I insist," I said.

"Give us a donation online or something," Wes countered. "My mom already said I'm not allowed to charge you."

"When did you even talk to your mom?" I protested.

"I texted her just a minute ago," he said matter-of-factly.

"You do have to fill out the adoption paperwork, though. She said it's the only way we can officially pass on ownership."

"What are you going to name her?" Tiffany asked as she approached and trailed her fingertips over the dog's back.

I looked down at her, cocking my head to the side. "Honey." As if she understood, the dog nudged my knee.

Tiffany grinned, replying, "Perfect."

———

That night, Honey scarfed down her meal and then climbed on the couch with me. She curled up beside me, watching television alertly. With Tiffany waiting in the SUV on the way back from the rescue program, I'd swung by the grocery store and cruised the pet section for a dog bed, collar, leash, a few toys, and food.

"You're all set," I said a bit later as I put the dog bed on the floor beside my bed.

It was a giant fluffy bed. Honey clambered into it, happily nuzzling in after circling several times.

The following morning, I found myself looking over toward Jonah's place. I knew he was gone, and I couldn't help but experience a little pang in my chest. I scoffed mentally. *He's just your neighbor. So what if you've kissed him twice? It means nothing.*

Yet I liked knowing he was there through the trees and missed his presence.

Chapter Fifteen

JONAH

A gust of wind blew a blast of heat and smoke toward me. I turned my face away, staying focused. As if on cue, I heard the distinct sound of a helicopter ahead and looked up to see one approaching and dropping fire retardant as another followed with water.

I kept at my work, clearing underbrush steadily. We'd been dealing with this fire and creating a perimeter deep in the wilderness. The fire was threatening a nearby rural community. Although the wind had been fighting us, it was finally changing direction, so we hoped to get a clear perimeter established in the next day or so.

I heard a voice and glanced back to see Chase approaching. He called over, "River up ahead. Let's keep working until we get across it."

"You got it."

A few hours later, I leaned back on my elbows on the ground, looking toward the sky. Rain was falling steadily now. I glanced toward Graham, commenting, "What's the scoop on this rain?"

He flashed a grin as he dragged a sleeve across his

forehead. "It's gonna do us a big favor. Slow and steady for the next day or so."

"Nice!" Rowan called from where he sat on the ground nearby.

After days of hard work, smoke, and heat, it was a relief to just relax in the light falling rain.

"We're actually going to head out in the next hour or two," Graham added. "I already radioed for a pickup."

I grinned, pushing off my elbows to sit up and snag a granola bar out of my backpack. A few hours later, I was gritting my teeth and breathing through the pain.

"I fucking dislocated my knee," I muttered to Graham.

"It happens," he said laconically.

"Not to me."

"Would you prefer something else?" Nate asked dryly from the pilot's seat.

I let out a sigh. "I suppose not. It just seems like, I don't know..."

"A lame injury?" Russell offered from the seat beside me.

I glanced at him, rolling my eyes. "Maybe not lame."

Rowan chuckled from where he sat in front of me. He twisted sideways to meet my eyes. "You'll be fine. It hurts like hell, though."

"Have you ever dislocated a knee before?" I asked

"Oddly enough, once in high school. I used to do track, and I landed weird over one of the jumps."

I glanced down at my leg stretched out in front of me. When I'd been helping load the gear in the helicopter, we'd realized one of the gear packs was missing. I had jumped out to get it. My foot landed on a rock, and I stumbled, dislocating my knee in the process. It fucking hurt like hell.

Rowan and Graham had put it back in place, and now it was throbbing. I took a breath, letting it out slowly. All we had for painkillers was ibuprofen. In all honesty, that was all I wanted. I'd heard enough horror stories about opiates to avoid them for the rest of my life. I'd iced it. Graham insisted that I get checked out at the hospital when we got back.

"How long will it be before I'm back up to speed?" I asked Rowan.

"I don't know. For me, the swelling went down pretty quick, but I couldn't run track for the rest of the season. We only had a month left then. They had me do some physical therapy to strengthen the joint. Never happened again," he offered with a shrug.

"Fuck," I muttered.

Graham cast me a rueful grin. "Your timing is good. You know we're headed into winter soon."

"I guess I'll be grateful for small favors."

Maybe an hour or so later, I was being wheeled in by wheelchair into the hospital. I'd argued against the wheelchair, but Graham insisted on it, declaring he didn't want me making it worse. Even though I wasn't about to admit it, I didn't want to put any weight on my knee. It hurt like hell every time I did.

Graham stopped at the circular desk in the ER. It so happened Holly Fox was there. She looked up, glancing back and forth between us. "I'm assuming Jonah is the injured party here."

"Of course, he is. He's in the wheelchair," Graham said dryly. "He dislocated his knee. We just need him cleared."

Holly rounded the desk, coasting her concerned gaze over me. "Did Charlie send you guys this way?"

Graham nodded. "Yeah, she's all booked at the office. She said you guys can do it as an acute care visit. I don't even know the difference."

Holly nodded along. "While you came into the ER, we have the walk-in clinic for her family practice in one of the wings." Holly gestured toward a hallway. "One of her medical assistants will take a look, and we'll go from there." She glanced at me. "By the way, your grandmother is going to be okay."

"What?!" I barked.

"You didn't know she was here?" Her brown eyes widened.

"Uh, no. What are you talking about?"

"Let me take you to her. In the meantime, I'll page Rachel."

"Who is Rachel, and who is Charlie, by the way?" I asked.

"She'll fill you in. I need to get back to the station. Holly, make sure they give me an update," Graham called as he backed up with a wave.

"Of course!" Holly called over her shoulder as she turned the wheelchair and began moving me down the hallway.

"What happened to Gram?" I repeated.

"She's fine, but she passed out this morning. Dennis couldn't get her in his car, so he went over to Alice's, and she drove her in. I don't know why he didn't call the ambulance, not that it matters. I don't think they could've gotten her here any sooner. She's fine. She's just, well—" Holly stopped and turned to face me. "You know she's dying, right?"

I felt as if I were falling and took a quick breath. "Today?" I was on my grandmother's approved list of contacts with her doctor and the hospital, so beyond what she'd told me, I knew her odds weren't good.

"Not today, but she's slowing down. She felt really weak so we've got her on an IV to get her fluids up. The doctor thinks she is dehydrated. She needs to do a better job of staying on top of that. Charlie's in surgery, but she checked her out this morning. She'll make some adjustments so your grandmother is more comfortable at home."

My heart gave an achy beat. Holly started wheeling me again. Moments later, I was in the hospital room, studying my grandmother. She rolled her head to the side, immediately asking, "Why are you in a wheelchair?"

"I dislocated my knee. Stupid injury. I was jumping down to get something and landed on a rock. It was just a bad landing," I explained. "The more important question is how are you?"

Gram narrowed her eyes, completely ignoring my question. "You are not allowed to get hurt," she announced, wagging a finger at me.

A chuckle rustled in my throat. "I did get hurt, but I'm fine. How are you?"

Gram waved a hand dismissively in the air. "I am fine. Dennis didn't even need to bring me here."

Holly checked something on the screen on the monitor beside my grandmother, clucking as she looked at her. "Dennis did the right thing by calling Alice. Your fluids were low, and you passed out. We want you comfortable and preferably conscious."

"I'm dying," Gram said, appearing annoyed by the whole thing.

I shook my head slowly, my heart giving several achy thumps. "Maybe you are dying," I offered, "but we want you comfortable. I'm glad Dennis asked Alice to drive you here."

"Well, I'm here for the night. Charlie already said

so. How are you going to get home? I don't think you can drive with that." She gestured toward my right leg.

"Oh shit. I didn't even think about that."

"Give me my phone," she barked at Holly who laughed softly as she handed the phone over from where it sat on a nearby table. "Alice will pick you up. Have you even been checked out yet?"

I rolled my eyes. "No, I just got here."

Holly glanced over at her, offering, "I wanted him to see you first. I've already paged Rachel because Charlie's in surgery. Rachel will check him out and probably do an X-ray to make sure it's just dislocated, and he didn't tear anything. After that, we'll send him home. We can rustle someone up if Alice can't give him a ride."

Only a few minutes later, Gram was shooing me out of her room. After what felt like hours later, Holly stopped in to check on me. I eyed her skeptically. "What now?"

"Nothing," she said with a quick smile. "I'm only checking on you because you're my friend. I'm the supervisor here in the ER, you know."

"I know, and I'm sure you're a kick-ass nurse and supervisor. I just want to go home," I said bluntly.

She flashed a grin. "You're cleared for discharge. Your knee will be sore as hell for a few days and then sort of sore for a little bit longer. You're in luck, though. You didn't tear any ligaments," she offered with a quick shrug. "Charlie is already dealing with another surgery because she's on call today, but she told me to check with you about pain medication."

"I just want strong ibuprofen. The most powerful dose available."

"You sure you don't want something else?" she pressed with her hands on her hips.

"Fuck, no. It *is* sore, but ibuprofen will do the trick."

"I'd recommend alternating ibuprofen and acetaminophen."

"Why?" I barked, catching myself and letting out a sigh at my sharp tone. "Sorry. I'm just ready to get home and get comfortable."

Unperturbed, Holly simply answered my question. "Because they're different pain medications. By alternating them, you can have pain relief more consistently. I'll send you home with some, and you can get more for yourself. If that's not enough—" I shook my head, and she held a finger up. "Let me finish, please." I smiled, circling my hand in the air for her to continue. "If that's not enough, just give Charlie's office a call tomorrow. You can't drive," she pointed out for what felt like the hundredth time between her and Rachel and another nurse who'd checked in with me.

"I know. Rachel said I can't drive for two weeks, at least."

"Well, you're timing is good. Alice stopped by to check on your grandmother. I told her you would need a ride home, so she's in the waiting area."

Holly turned and reached for a pair of crutches that I hadn't even noticed were propped against the door. I started to shake my head, and she rolled her eyes. I stood on my own and limped over. "It's sore, but I really don't need crutches."

"I'll put them in the back of Alice's SUV. This way, if you find yourself in worse shape tomorrow morning, you've got something to help you hobble around."

A short while later, Holly was standing at the curb outside of the hospital and peering into the passenger side window of Alice's SUV. "He's all set. He's got ibuprofen and acetaminophen to alternate. The crutches are in the back. I know his grandmother would check on him in the morning, but since she's here, I think you should."

I glanced back and forth between them, rolling my eyes. "Could I please just go home?" I asked as nicely as I could.

Chapter Sixteen

JONAH

Holly stepped back from the curb. "Yes, you can. Don't overdo it," she ordered.

A moment later, Alice was driving. She glanced over when she came to a stop before turning onto Main Street. "It takes forever to do hardly anything at the hospital, doesn't it?" Her tone was warm and understanding.

The tension bundled tightly inside me started to uncoil. "Yes," I simply said. Alice's new rescue dog, Honey, who was in the back seat with the crutches I didn't intend to use, leaned forward and nuzzled my shoulder. I scratched her behind the ears, and my lips tugged into a smile at the sound of her tail thumping against the seat.

Alice's lips quirked with another smile as she turned, adding, "You'll be sore, but it sounds like you'll be fine. It's Holly's job to tell you all the things."

"I know."

We drove in silence for a few minutes before I spoke again. "Thank you for taking Gram to the hospital this morning."

"Of course!" Alice exclaimed. "It sounds like they're keeping her for the night."

"Yeah, they want to monitor her vitals for the night and get her fluids up. I feel like I should've noticed something," I said, a twinge of guilt stinging my heart.

"I see her almost every day too, and I didn't notice anything. She's never been one to complain about not feeling well, which isn't the best trait when you have terminal cancer."

I couldn't help but chuckle because that was the gentlest possible way for her to describe my grandmother. She never complained and *definitely* didn't want to ask for help.

"That's pretty on the nose. I'm glad Dennis is there to keep an eye on her."

"Yeah, I am too."

"Every so often, I wonder if I should ask about staying at the main house."

"Do you think she'd want that?" Alice asked.

I cast her a grin. "No way. I asked before, and she told me I would cramp her style."

Alice burst out laughing. "Well, you would. They *are* newlyweds, after all."

We laughed together, and the rest of the ride was quiet. My knee wasn't that painful, just sore.

After Alice parked, she ran to the back of the SUV and fetched the crutches. Because I was a stubborn asshole, I climbed out, testing my knee carefully once I stood.

Alice studied me. "Are you sure you don't want to use the crutches?"

"Fuck no," I said flatly.

She pressed her lips in a line, but her throaty laughter slipped out anyway as she shrugged. "All right. Well, I'll carry them just in case."

We began walking, and my stomach let out an audible growl.

"When's the last time you had anything to eat?" she asked.

I mentally skimmed through the day, eventually replying, "I had a granola bar before we got on the helicopter."

"You're coming with me," she ordered. "I'm making you some dinner."

"You don't have to—" I began.

Alice came to a stop on the path and turned to face me, pointing one of the crutches at me. "I'm making you dinner. You've been gone for over a week. I'm guessing you don't have much in your fridge, and you've had a long day. It's not that late."

I hadn't even paid attention to the time and finally glanced at my watch, realizing it was only seven o'clock. Feeling sheepish, I smiled over at her. "Are you sure you don't mind?"

"Of course, I don't mind."

Honey gamely bounced along the side of us on her three legs. I glanced down as she darted into the trees to sniff something before quickly returning to Alice's side.

"How long did you say you had her?"

"I got her from the shelter this week. Somebody dumped her at the end of the road," she said, letting out an annoyed puff.

"You're not worried about her running off?"

I watched as the dog darted into the trees again, returning to Alice's side after sniffing the base of one thoroughly.

Alice looked from the dog to me and grinned. "No, I'm not. She's kind of stuck to me. I've been taking her into the office. The only problem is she wants to go everywhere with me, even to the exam room. That's not cool because sometimes the other pets get stressed out." She leaned down to stroke her palm across the dog's back, adding, "We'll work on some training once she's more comfortable."

Not much later, Alice had me situated in her kitchen at the table. I had my leg propped up on a pillow on a chair and one of the sports gel packs that Holly had sent home over my knee. I didn't think I needed it, but Alice insisted, telling me she didn't want to lie to my grandmother or Holly if they asked if I did what I was supposed to.

My mind skipped tracks, something I hated. The last time I'd been in a hospital and then home recovering from injuries was after the shooting. My parents and my grandmother hadn't been able to get there in time for my first night at home. I remembered feeling so raw inside, with the pains from my actual injuries the least of my worries. Even thinking about it now, there was this almost echo of a pain where I'd been shot, a stinging percussive sensation.

I forcefully nudged my mind away from that track. That was over. I was here, now, in a place where, well, where people took care of each other.

"I'm assuming you like salmon?" Alice asked.

I brought my attention to her. She stood by the counter with one hand resting on it. Her hair was pulled up in a messy ponytail with loose curls framing her face. She wore a pair of leggings with a tank top and an open button-down shirt. The fabric of her tank top was stretched tight across her breasts.

What was becoming a familiar feeling sizzled to life inside me. Alice was fucking sexy as hell, and I wanted her. A distant voice in my brain pointed out that I was just seeking a distraction. *So what?* I silently scoffed.

"Jonah?" she prompted.

Oh right, she had asked me an actual question. "Of course, I like salmon."

"Well, that settles it, then. I'll make something quick. I'll cook it under the broiler with a lemon-honey glaze and a little bit of pepper." As if in reply, my stomach growled. She grinned. "Sound good?"

"Sounds fucking great."

"Would you like a beer? Or wine?" She tossed those questions over her shoulder as she turned to open the refrigerator.

"I'll take a beer."

She reeled off several types from a local brewery in Diamond Creek.

"Wow, you have a selection."

She cast me another smile over her shoulder, and the twinkle in her eyes sent a shot of blood straight to my cock. "I like good beer and wine."

"I'll take the honey porter."

I savored my beer while Alice cooked dinner. We ate together at her table in the cozy kitchen, and I tried not to think too much about how I enjoyed this simple time—just relaxing in her kitchen with the moon rising over the mountains and casting a pearly shimmer across the lake. It all felt, well, rather domestic.

Restless with that train of thought, I let my greedy gaze linger on the curves of her breasts. She cleared her throat, and my eyes whipped up to hers. Pink stained her cheeks, and when my eyes dipped down again, her nipples were tight little peaks.

"This was excellent," I said as I finished my last bite.

Alice had whipped up a quick batch of seasoned rice along with the salmon. It was a simple but delicious meal.

She looked pleased as she pushed her plate toward the center of the table and leaned back in her chair. "I agree. I'm glad you enjoyed it."

She reached for her wineglass and drained the last of it. After she set the glass on the table, her fingers traced along the stem idly. Meanwhile, I shifted in my chair. I'd been half aroused for hours at this point.

Chapter Seventeen

ALICE

Jonah's gaze lifted to mine, and my hormones did a little dance. I had honestly offered to cook him dinner because, for obvious reasons, he'd had a long day. I hadn't intended for it to be an evening that was one long tease of foreplay.

I was grateful Honey was sound asleep on her new favorite perch, her bed in the hallway. Sometime during her first night here, she'd dragged the bed just outside my bedroom door, so I left it there. She seemed to like it because she could keep an eye on me in the bedroom but also see out into the living room and through the windows.

I was acutely aware of the damp silk between my thighs.

"How does your knee feel?" I asked, desperate for any distraction. I was in bad enough shape that my voice came out raspy and a little breathless. I hoped he didn't notice. I also hoped he didn't notice that my nipples were tight, so tight they ached. It felt as if they were announcing my state, waving and cheering for his attention.

He lifted a shoulder in an easy shrug. "Not bad. A little sore. It's an annoying injury, and I feel like an idiot, but all things considered, I'll take it."

"Why do you feel like an idiot? It could've happened to anyone," I pointed out.

"Because I'm a man. Even if I know that's stupid, it just feels ridiculous that I stepped on a rock, but it was enough of a distance on the descent that I landed wrong."

"You'll be fine," I assured him. "I'm sure your ego will recover from this blow."

He spun his empty beer bottle with his fingers, and I clenched my thighs together. My body seemed to have a mind of its own. I wanted Jonah, and I wanted his hands all over me. I wanted to know every inch of him and him to know every inch of me.

We stared at each other, and I thought, maybe, I saw the answering flare of desire in his eyes. Restless, I stood from my chair, lifting my plate and his and carrying them to the sink. I rinsed them quickly and put them in the dishwasher.

I heard a motion and turned to see that he had stood and crossed over to toss his beer bottle in the recycling bin under the counter. He lifted my empty wine glass. "Dishwasher?"

At my nod, he put it in the dishwasher and turned to close it. I stood by the counter, with my hands curled over the edge and my heartbeat echoing through my body. I was hot all over, my skin tingling as I looked at him.

Jonah crossed the kitchen to me, his steps slow. He was clearly favoring his left leg, and I asked, "Should you be on your feet?"

He stopped in front of me, placing one hand and

then the other beside my hips, each movement purposeful and deliberate. "I'm fine."

With his green gaze boring into mine, I could hardly catch my breath. His eyes searched mine for a moment before he said, "I want you, Alice."

I let out a startled gasp. "Well, that was blunt," I sputtered.

"I thought maybe I should just get right to the point," he said, his voice low and gravelly.

Shivers raced through me, and I felt myself arching like a cat when he dipped his head and dropped a hot kiss on the side of my neck. I let out a little whimper, and then he dropped another hot kiss on the soft skin below my jaw. I bit my lip and couldn't hold back my moan.

He proceeded to make love to the sweet spot along the side of my neck, driving me to distraction in the process. When I whimpered his name, he lifted his head. At the loss of his lips on my skin, I felt bereft, as if he had stolen something from me.

We stared at each other, the air charged with desire. He lifted a hand, brushing the loose curls away from my cheek. "Tell me what you want, Alice."

I swallowed and tried to take a breath while my heart rampaged in my chest, wild and out of control. I licked my lips before answering with the plain and simple truth. "You." I placed my palm on his chest, almost relieved to feel his heart kicking hard and fast. Belatedly, I added, "But you're hurt."

His eyes skated over my face, dipping down. My nipples tightened in response when his gaze lifted to mine again. "Not really."

His mouth claimed me with a devouring kiss. I didn't have time to think. I didn't want to think.

Jonah was a commanding kisser. My knees were

weak and wobbly. I felt as if I were melting with every bold stroke of his tongue against mine. His hand slid to cup the back of my neck, his thumb brushing along the sensitive skin right behind my ear. Every touch sent a shower of sensation raining through me.

Just when I thought I could barely take it anymore and I was desperate for air, he broke free, leaning his head back and sucking in a deep breath. I gulped in several breaths. We stared at each other in the light cast over the sink.

His hand loosened at the back of my neck, and he lifted it, murmuring, "Can I take this out?" He tugged lightly on the elastic holding my hair in a ponytail.

Wordlessly, I nodded. The feel of his fingers tugging it free sent a shiver over my scalp and down my spine. He tossed it on the counter before sliding his fingers through my hair.

My eyes fell closed as I took a breath. I didn't know what it was about Jonah and the effect he had on me, but every touch sent fire spinning through me, the flames licking higher and higher inside. The scorching heat of need threatened to engulf me.

I dragged my eyes open, and we stared at each other. I could hear the rush of blood with every drumming beat of my heart. Before I could think further, his hand slid free of my curls, reaching for one of mine as he tugged me away from the counter.

"Where —?" I began.

My question was cut off by his mouth as he tugged me close, spinning me around. We were moving, and I broke free to protest, "Your knee!"

He ignored me. His gait was uneven, but in another moment, we were in the living room. He sat down on the couch, pulling me onto his lap. I discovered I could kiss Jonah perhaps forever. One kiss melted into the next. I didn't know when it happened, but I was straddling him, rocking over the hard ridge of his arousal. The friction of the fabric between us tightened the sensations spinning through me. I felt like a string being pulled taut to the point it may snap.

"Slow down," he murmured against my throat.

I shivered, arching into him, savoring the feel of his teeth grazing along the sensitive skin at the base of my throat. "I can't!" I gasped as he cupped a breast, his fingers teasing lightly over my ruched nipple.

He chuckled, lifting his head and palming my cheek. His thumb traced along my bottom lip, and I couldn't resist nipping at it. His hips rocked upward into mine.

In another moment, his hand dropped away, and he pushed my blouse off my shoulders, murmuring, "I need to see you."

"You've already seen me naked," I teased.

His gaze lifted to mine as he hooked a palm under the hem of my tank top, pushing it up and letting it ride up his wrists. "Not good enough. That was defi-nitely at a distance," he whispered gruffly as he pushed my tank top up over my breasts.

I lifted my arms, and he whipped it up over my head where it fell with a rumple on the floor.

"Oh, sweetheart," he murmured reverently, his palms lightly cupping both breasts.

I needed more. I needed to feel his bare skin against mine. All I could say was, "Jonah, more."

Somehow, he knew just what I needed. He had my bra undone in a flash and tossed it aside, murmuring something indecipherable before I felt the warmth of both palms cupping my bare breasts. I arched into his touch, letting out a ragged whimper.

On the heels of a shaky breath, he was dipping his

head, and I felt the wet heat of his mouth closing over one needy nipple. He teased the other with his thumb and forefinger as he swirled his tongue and gave a sharp suck. The sensation rippled through me, narrowing to my very core as I clenched.

My hands were greedy, and I yanked at the hem of his shirt. He leaned back, giving me an assist as he lifted it in a swoop, up and over his head, where it fell beside my tank top. His warm muscled chest with a light dusting of auburn hair pressed against me as his hand slid up my spine, bringing his mouth to mine again.

A moment later, he broke free, growling, "Fuck me, Alice."

We stared at each other as I tried to catch my breath. It felt as if something snapped loose inside. I didn't know how to slow it down. I didn't want to. "We could get to that part," I rasped, half-teasing and also entirely serious.

Jonah's lips curled up at one corner. "We'll get there."

He smoothed my hair back, his hands sliding over my shoulders and down along my sides. I felt as if he were memorizing my shape. I let my fingers trail lightly over his muscled chest. As my eyes dipped down, it was impossible not to see the scars on his side.

Startled, I lifted my eyes to his. My questions caught in my throat.

He was quiet, and something dark flickered in his gaze. I thought I saw a flicker of pain in his eyes for a second, but it disappeared quickly.

He lifted a hand, catching one of my curls and spinning it around his finger as he replied, "I was shot at a school shooting." His words were flat, almost rote.

My heartbeat stuttered for a moment. My hand stilled where it rested on his chest. Even though I'd heard about the shooting, seeing the evidence of it slammed into me. "Jonah," I breathed as a sense of worry, momentary panic, and sadness struck me abruptly.

"It's okay," he assured me. "Obviously, I survived."

Emotions tumbled through me. I had so many questions, but none of them seemed right for this moment.

His gaze was steady when he added, "I don't want to dwell on it."

I nodded, whispering, "I'm sorry."

His eyes closed, opening on the heels of a deep breath. "Everyone's sorry."

I felt the beat of his heart under my palm, a little unsteady and fast. His fingers slid free of my curls, and he lightly caught my chin with his thumb dragging across my bottom lip again as he said, "Let's forget it for now."

Once again, Jonah made me forget everything except the need rushing through me. The force was so intense it knocked everything free inside like a river breaking through a dam in the spring.

Later, I would think that something about seeing his scars and learning what happened had intensified all of it. Yet at this moment, all I knew were the sensations layering upon each other and how desperate I was to touch him, to feel him, to taste him.

He nudged me off his lap, ordering, "I want to see you naked. All of you."

I was happy to oblige and quickly stripped off my clothes. I was impatient because I wanted to see him too. With nimble fingers, I unbuttoned his jeans. He lifted his hips as I tugged them down along with his briefs.

His cock was long and thick. I curled a palm around it, teasing my thumb over the tip where a drop of pre-cum rolled out. "Condom," he bit out.

He shifted and snagged his jeans off the floor, shaking until his wallet fell out. In a matter of seconds, he was rolling a condom on.

A moment later, I was straddling him again, savoring the feel of the underside of his cock sliding between my slippery wet folds.

"Slow down," he murmured again.

I stared at him, my mouth half open. I felt my heartbeat in the very core of me.

He shifted me back, bringing his fingers between my thighs. His eyes were on mine the entire time as he slipped two inside me, stretching, almost testing to see if I was ready for him.

I was more than ready. My hips bucked against his hand as he drew out and then pumped inside me with his fingers. "Almost there, sweetheart."

I needlessly asked, "Is your knee okay?"

"Not thinking about it. All I notice is you."

He drew his fingers out, and I watched as he lifted them and sucked them into his mouth, murmuring, "You taste so good."

I swallowed, my pussy clenching. "I need you inside me," I said tightly.

I wasn't usually this demanding, but with Jonah, it was as if my restraint had broken free. His hands gripped my hips. As I rose, he reached between us, positioning his cock at my entrance, whispering, "Easy now."

I felt the thick press of his crown sliding inside, stretching me. He controlled the slow descent of my hips as I lowered over him, sheathing him inside my slick core. A moan escaped when he was finally seated fully inside. I wiggled my hips as if in emphasis.

We were completely still through several resounding beats of my heart. Then he nudged deeper. I rose again, sinking down slowly, savoring the stretch.

My breasts brushed against his chest with every roll of our hips together. The slippery fusion where we were joined teased against my clit, sending sharp, piercing jolts of pleasure through me. With every breath, I was chasing my release as it built to a crescendo inside, the sensation drawing tighter and tighter. He teased his fingers over my swollen clit. I thought I couldn't bear the pressure inside until it shattered, and I cried out, pleasure splintering through me, so sharp it was almost painful, so intense I lost sight of everything. My mind simply went blank.

All I knew was the feel of his arms holding me and the sensation breaking in sharp ripples through me.

Chapter Eighteen

JONAH

Alice was trembling against me. Her skin was soft and dewy, and my release had been threatening ever since I filled her. I rocked my hips once more, nudging just a little deeper into her clenching core and that was it. Lightning sizzled through me, the sensation was electric and intense.

She relaxed against me a moment later, her head tucking into the curve of my neck. I held her close, just trying to catch my breath. I idly sifted my fingers through her curls, savoring the feel of her breath gusting lightly against my skin.

After a few moments, I felt her lift her head, and I dragged my eyes open. We stared quietly at each other. Her silvery-gray eyes were serious as she studied me. She surprised me by leaning forward and pressing a kiss to the base of my throat. Her eyes fell closed, and I felt the breath she drew in, a subtle tightening in her body followed by release when she let it out. Her lashes lifted, and her eyes searched mine.

She seemed to be trying to think of what to say. I found myself caught in uncertainty for a moment. Just then, the sound of a dog's claws on the hardwood floor reached us.

Alice glanced over her shoulder, a smile stretching across her face when she looked back at me. "Saved by a three-legged dog."

I chuckled. "Did we need to be saved?"

Her gaze sobered, and she lifted her hand, trailing her fingertips along the stubbled edge of my jaw. "Maybe, maybe not."

We untangled ourselves. It was only then that the pain in my knee drew my attention as I gingerly walked to the bathroom to dispose of the condom and clean up. Alice glanced at me after I finished tugging my T-shirt back on as I returned to the living room. She gestured toward my leg, asking, "How does it feel?"

I looked at her for a long moment, savoring her tousled curls, the pink flush on her cheeks, and her kiss-swollen lips. "Well?" she prompted.

"It's sore. I think you helped me forget for a little bit." I eased my hips back on the couch.

Her lips twitched as she turned, crossing into the kitchen and rummaging through her purse, which sat on the corner of the counter. A moment later, she approached me. Honey's chin was resting on my good knee.

She held a glass of water aloft and two pills in her hand. "Holly gave me the medicine. She said your last dose was acetaminophen, so this is ibuprofen. You're supposed to alternate."

"She gave you that?"

Alice nodded. "You were right there. I think you were annoyed, so you didn't notice. Not with her, but the situation."

I took the glass of water and ibuprofen. "Thank

you." I swallowed the pills, chasing them with a gulp of water. "And you're right. It was the situation, not Holly. Thank you again for the ride."

Alice cocked her head to the side, resting her hands on her hips as she surveyed me. "You know all you have to do is ask."

"For what?"

She threw a hand in the air, letting it fall with a soft thump against the side of her thigh. "For anything. A ride, a cup of sugar. A ride for your grandmother. Things like that."

My heart twisted, a little sharply and a little sweetly in my chest as I looked up at this woman.

"The same goes for you," I replied huskily.

She reached for the water glass, taking it from me. "I'm taking Honey out. She probably needs to pee." She turned and began walking toward the door. Honey gamely hopped after her in her funny little walk.

Alice turned when her hand was on the doorknob, hitting me with a stern look. "Don't go anywhere. I'll be back in just a few minutes."

If my leg wasn't throbbing, I probably would've gotten up and left, but I was tired, so fucking tired. I needed a shower. Not because of Alice. Hell, I savored the scent of her clinging to me. Typically, I would go back to the station and shower after we got back, but Graham had delivered me straight to the hospital. I wanted to let the hot water wash away my day and let my leg rest. The idea of walking the short distance from Alice's house to my place in the darkness wasn't the least bit appealing.

I told myself I was just following her orders when I propped my leg on her coffee table and leaned my head back on the couch.

It couldn't have been that long before I felt the

cool press of a dog's nose against my palm. I dragged my eyes open, lifting my head and glancing around groggily.

"You fell asleep." Alice stood in front of me again, her arms akimbo. "I think you need a shower," she announced.

I eyed her, still drowsy, teasing, "Do I smell?"

She rolled her eyes. "Not really. Maybe a little bit like trees and smoke, but I guess I like trees and smoke."

I chuckled when a wash of pink tinged her cheeks.

"Come on, I'll help you in." She held out her hands.

Curling my hands around hers, I stood, protesting with, "I can walk fine. I can shower fine."

"No need to be a tough guy," she said lightly.

She escorted me down a short hallway to the bathroom. She gestured to some shelves built into a small alcove. "There are plenty of towels, and the hot water here is great." Shadows chased in her eyes for a moment before she turned away.

She was about to close the door when Honey walked through and sat on the bath mat, looking up at me expectantly. Alice's gaze was bemused when she glanced between us. "I guess she wants to make sure all goes well. If you leave the door cracked open, she can get out if she wants."

Moments later with Honey curled up on the bathmat outside the shower, the hot water pounded down on my shoulders. As promised, the hot water here *was* great. Definitely a step up from the water heater in Gram's small cabin. It was decent there, but I was pretty sure the last time she'd updated any of the amenities was probably before I was born.

After lathering my hands thoroughly, I soaped my

body, my hand lingering over the scars on my side as it did every time I took a shower. It was almost as if I was reminding myself they were nothing more than surface scars. I'd always promised myself whenever anybody asked, I would just tell the truth, yet I hadn't counted on telling the truth to someone like Alice.

Or, rather, I hadn't expected Alice. Since the shooting, I was certain counting on anyone, or counting on life to cut you some slack, was asking too much.

Alice made me want to count on someone and for someone to count on me. I kicked those thoughts away, but they spun like a boomerang right back. Alice was steady, the kind of person you could count on.

Things are getting complicated, my cynical, bitter mind pointed out.

No, they're not. She's just my neighbor.

Just a woman whose flame burned so bright I couldn't look away. Just a woman who, in a very short time, I already felt closer to than anyone I'd ever dated. And we weren't even dating. A few kisses and the hottest encounter of my life.

When I turned off the water, Honey was waiting, and she blinked up at me, her tail thumping on the floor. She hadn't mastered getting up quickly, and it took more than one try. I wondered what had happened to her leg. Alice had pointed out someone had paid for the surgery, and then she got dumped. She'd told me they'd checked the records at the clinic, and the surgery hadn't happened there.

Honey followed me to the kitchen, where Alice was wiping the counter. Alice turned, her eyes skating over me before she said, "I think you should stay here."

I didn't even know what to think of the intense

wash of relief and emotion that flowed through me. I didn't want to leave.

"You think?" I returned, keeping my tone light.

She nodded. "Your grandmother will give me hell if I let you walk through those trees in the dark."

We studied each other for a long moment, and then her lips curled into a smile as she shrugged. I chuckled softly, replying, "Absolutely."

Chapter Nineteen

ALICE

The rhythm of Jonah's breathing was deep and even. Within a minute of me tugging the covers up over us, he'd fallen asleep. He had to be exhausted after a week out in the backcountry fighting a wildfire.

Meanwhile, thoughts were pinging in my mind. With all that I had just allowed to happen with Jonah, my brain chased worries in circles. I had wanted him, wanted what I felt with him, and had grabbed it with both hands. Even now, in the quiet darkness with him beside me and Honey curled up on her new favorite bed nearby, I got hot all over just thinking about it.

I didn't expect Jonah. I also didn't expect how I felt with him. In all honesty, I was accustomed to being let down when it came to sex. Chemistry didn't mean much of anything, or so I thought. Until Jonah. With us, it felt like one flame leaping into the next, the fire burning hotter and hotter.

My mind spun to the scars on his side and the shocking cause. There were school shootings in the news so often that it was easy to feel inured to them. Having grown up in Alaska with parents who hunted alongside the basic risks of living on the edge of the wilderness, I'd been around guns my entire life and knew how to handle them. One was kept tucked on a shelf in the closet right by the door. It had been there as long as I could remember because one year we had problems with a black bear who had her cubs nearby. My father taught me how to use it in case I needed to scare her off.

But school shootings? My very being recoiled at the thought of it. My heart felt cracked to realize Jonah had survived one.

I had so many questions. Yet I knew from the look on his face when I'd noticed his scars that it wasn't my place to ask. I curled onto my side, studying his profile. The moonlight fell through the window, casting the angles of his face in a silvery relief. I wanted to trace my fingertips along his cheekbone and lightly draw over his sensual mouth. But he needed to sleep, and I wanted that for him.

———

"Jonah," I breathed.

Steam billowed around us as the water rained down in the shower.

"Yes?" he drawled.

His palm slid down to tease over my nipple, slippery from the soap he'd just rubbed all over me.

"Your knee," I protested weakly.

I'd gotten a good look at his knee this morning. It was barely swollen. He told me it ached, but that was it.

"My knee is fine," he murmured as his palm slid over the curve of my belly and dipped between my thighs.

I gasped when he sank two fingers inside me.

Jonah was blowing all of my low expectations about sex to smithereens. After I'd taken Honey for her morning walk and fed her breakfast, he caught me by the hand and tugged me into the shower.

I cried out, arching back as he pumped his fingers skillfully in and out of me. In another moment, he turned, seating himself on the corner shelf in the shower. It was a nice shower with two rainfall shower-heads above and additional ones mounted on the walls. There was a bench just outside of the fall of the water on one side. He sat down, stretching his leg out. His arousal jutted up, and my body clenched in response.

"See, I'm sitting down," he teased as he pulled me to him. He'd thought ahead and reached for the condom on the shelf nearby, opening it and rolling it on swiftly.

I couldn't help it. I *needed* him inside me. I craved the feeling of him filling me. When I knelt over him and sank down, my body trembled as my release raced through me. He was as primed as I was, thrusting into me with several deep surges before I felt the press of his fingers on my hip. With one arm wrapped around my waist, I felt the heat of his release spurting inside me.

When I opened my eyes, my heart felt jolted by the shock of intimacy. He gave me a lingering kiss and then helped me up. The rest of our shower was entirely practical.

Jonah was solicitous, handing me a towel after we got out. I worried when I saw the subtle hitch in his gait as he walked out of the bathroom a few minutes later.

I made omelets with smoked salmon and cream

cheese. After we finished eating, his phone rang, and I turned away, busying myself with cleaning up.

"Everything okay?" I asked when he set his phone on the table a moment later.

He looked up. "That was the hospital. Gram's okay. They plan to discharge her later this afternoon after running a few more tests."

"Do you want me to give her a ride?"

Chapter Twenty

JONAH

"What kind of tests?" I asked Dennis.

"They originally said they'd discharge her this morning, but they want to run some kind of test on her heart."

My own heart twisted with worry. I had intellectually accepted my grandmother's choice not to go through another round of treatment for her cancer.

Yet my mind's rational acceptance didn't erase the emotional pain. Grief was waiting in the wings.

"I'm surprised she's letting them run any tests," I said dryly.

Dennis chuckled, the sound holding a sharp edge to it. "I know. She said she wants to be comfortable."

"Alice already said she'd give her a ride home."

"I like Alice," Dennis offered. "She's solid."

"Solid?"

He grinned. "Yeah, solid. The kind of woman you want to settle down with."

I cocked my head to the side, studying him for a few beats. "I'm not looking for someone to settle down with."

"Yeah, I know. Because you're a dumbass. The fact you wondered what I meant proves my point."

I pressed my tongue into my cheek as a dry laugh rustled in my throat. "Oh, so you weren't talking about me?"

"Yeah, I was, but my point is you thinking I was is what means something."

I took a breath, letting it out in a quick sigh. "Dennis, I'm not cut out for romance."

"Your Gram thinks otherwise. She said she saw you two kissing," he pointed out.

I pressed my lips together and shook my head. "It was a kiss. That doesn't mean I'm settling down or even thinking about it."

I couldn't even believe I was having this fucking conversation with my grandmother's new husband. My grandmother was dying, but that clearly didn't stem her tendency to nose into my business.

"I expected Gram to be nosy, but not you," I pointed out.

Dennis shrugged, unabashed. "Why do you think we love each other?"

I chuckled. "Good point."

Dennis was quiet as he finished off a piece of toast. After Alice had gone to work, I stopped by my place to change clothes before making my way over to check on Dennis with a minor limp. He was having toast and poached eggs for breakfast.

"I know you don't like to talk about it..." he began.

"Talk about what?"

"The shooting," he offered calmly.

My heart started pounding. For a second, I thought I was going to break out in a cold sweat right here in front of Dennis.

I took a slow breath, and the icy feeling inside

started to dissipate. I had begun to notice the horrible feeling didn't last as long whenever I thought about that day. "What do you mean?"

"I went to war. I know something about things you'd prefer to forget, things you'd prefer never to have happened. Some of my friends came home and got drunk for years. Some came home and buried themselves in whatever—work, life. Some of us came home and drank for a little bit and then figured out it didn't help to get lost in it. I've been sober for forty years now. I know something about facing down bad memories. I promise you it gets easier. I'm not saying it'll be the same way for you as it is for me, but I *am* saying the only way to get through to the other side is to stop running. You know that, uh, thing. Fear." He circled his hand in the air.

"Fear?"

"I don't mean the word. The acronym," he clarified.

"What acronym?" I prompted.

"F-E-A-R," he spelled out. "Fear. Fuck everything and run, or face everything and recover," he said with a little shrug. "It's one or the other, no matter how you go about it."

I stared at him for a minute and then laughed softly as I shook my head. "Not a bad acronym."

He flashed a quick grin before his gaze sobered. "Your Gram's worried about you."

"I came to Alaska like she wanted," I pointed out.

"You did, but running isn't a geographical thing."

I took a slow breath, my mind spinning back to last night with Alice. I knew what he meant. "You know I was just dating her. We weren't serious."

Her being Tina, the guidance counselor who died in the shooting, who was dead while I tried to save whoever I could. I had liked Tina. Maybe it would've become more, but I never got the chance to find out.

Dennis nodded. "Sure, I know. But you think it's not worth it. That's all I'm saying. It's always worth it."

"Even marrying Gram, knowing she's going to die soon?"

"Hell yeah. About only one thing in life is guaranteed: we all die."

Chapter Twenty-One

JONAH

That afternoon, I climbed out of Nate's truck, glancing in before I closed the door. "Thanks for the ride, man."

"Anytime. Glad you're doing all right. When can you drive again?"

"Two weeks probably. I'm supposed to swing by and have Charlie clear me." I leaned my weight on my knee, testing it. "It really feels okay."

"Well, if you need another ride, just call me. Or walk down to Firehouse Café. You can find someone to give you a ride."

I grinned. "Good point."

I watched as Nate drove away, thinking it was nice to be in a place where I could walk down to the coffee shop, and somebody would likely offer me a ride.

I mulled that over later when I walked through the door to the vet clinic and looked around. The waiting room was full. Someone had a goat on a leash, an unhappy cat was in a carrier meowing rather dramatically, and someone else had a wiggly puppy in their lap. A woman I didn't recognize was at the reception desk, checking someone else out. I approached the desk, waiting.

After the person in front of me paid, the receptionist looked up. "You must be Jonah," she announced by way of greeting.

"Yeah," I said slowly.

"I'm not a weirdo. You don't have a pet, and Alice said to expect you. She's giving you a ride. Everybody in the waiting area is done. I just have to check them out. I'm Tiffany Mills," she explained, her dark hair swinging in its ponytail as she turned to set down some papers next to her.

I grinned. "Nice to meet you," I returned. "I'd introduce myself, but you already know I'm Jonah. The place is busy."

Her blue eyes brightened when she smiled up at me. "Exactly how we want it."

The cat let out another operatic wail, and Tiffany met my eyes, laughing softly. "Alice is in the back." She gestured to the door on the side of the reception desk. "Go on back."

The cat's wailing was muted as I walked into the hallway. I was about to call Alice's name when she appeared from a doorway toward the end of the short hall. She smiled when she saw me. "Hey, I wasn't sure if it was you or Tiffany." She watched as I approached, commenting, "Not much of a limp."

My lips tugged into a smile as I stopped in front of her. The urge to kiss her was almost overwhelming. "I see Charlie in two weeks, but I honestly think I'm okay to drive now."

She rested a hand on her hip, her eyes giving me a once-over. That now familiar electricity shimmied to life in the air around us, snapping and crackling. "Well, you're not driving on my watch. Come on in here." She gestured with her hands as she turned and walked through a doorway. I followed her in, glancing around. Shelves lined the walls, and a small table in the center had a laptop sitting on it.

"Finishing up for the day?" I prompted.

"Yeah." She tapped a few keys on the keyboard, waiting a moment before closing the laptop. "We're busy," she announced.

"I noticed the waiting area was full. Do you need to wait before we leave?"

She shook her head, slipping out of her white lab coat. "Nope. Tiffany's checking everybody out, and she'll lock up."

I followed her into a break room across the hallway, where she hung her lab coat in a small locker and fetched her purse and keys. A few moments later, we were driving toward the hospital in her car. "So how was your day?" she asked.

"Definitely not as busy as yours," I offered with a chuckle. "I had breakfast with Dennis and talked to my parents. They are planning to come up sooner."

"What do you mean?" She turned onto Main Street, asking, "Do you mind if I swing by Firehouse Café? I could use some coffee."

"Not at all. I'll get one myself. We should get something for Gram. She loves their hot chocolate."

"Perfect. Anyway, back to your parents. They're coming to visit?"

"Yeah. They were planning to come to visit no matter what for a little bit because..." I paused.

Alice filled in, "Bea is sick?"

"Exactly. They want to stay until she passes."

"It's really nice they can do that," she said, her tone soft.

"It is. My dad is a professor, and he can work

online. My mom's retired from teaching. They decided to bump their arrival up when they heard she went to the hospital."

Alice turned into the parking area at Firehouse Café, and we walked in a moment later. "Where will they stay?" she asked when we stopped at the back of the line.

"That's a good question. Gram's place isn't that big."

"Is her house where your dad grew up?" Alice asked as we waited.

"No. She had a bigger house with my grandfather, who passed when I was little."

"I don't even remember him," she said.

"He died when I was little, massive heart attack back in the days when they couldn't make people live forever," I explained.

"I'm sorry," Alice said quietly.

We stepped forward with the line as I replied, "Thank you. It's been a long time. After that, she decided to downsize, and that's when she bought the house where she lives and the cabin. She's been renting out the B&B for years."

"It's weird how people have lives before you know them, and it feels like what you knew was how it always was. All I remember is her being next door. It's like she's been there forever." She paused, glancing ahead. "Oh, it's us!" She bounced forward to the front of the line.

Janet was waiting behind the counter and smiled at us. "How's the knee?" she asked by way of greeting.

"How do you know about my knee?" I countered.

Janet grinned. "I know almost everything, plus Nate was just here and told me he dropped you off. He should've brought you here."

I chuckled. "Alice is taking me to pick up Gram. We're getting coffee and whatever Gram's favorite hot chocolate is."

"The peppermint," Janet said firmly. "And I don't have your usuals memorized. What can I get for you?"

"I'll just take the house coffee. It's plenty strong," I said.

"I'll take an Americano with a little bit of cream," Alice offered.

She reached to open her purse, and I slipped my wallet out of my pocket quickly. "This one's on me."

"Are you sure?"

"Absolutely. You gave me a ride home yesterday, and you're helping me pick up Gram tonight. This is the least I can do."

Janet grinned as she prepped our coffees. "How is Bea?" she asked.

"Good, I think. I talked to her today on the phone. She was annoyed they didn't let her loose this morning."

"You mean discharge her?" Alice prompted dryly.

"She called it being let loose. As far as I know, she feels fine. Apparently, she needs to stay hydrated. My parents are coming up early. They'll be here this weekend," I explained.

"Nice, Bea will love that," Janet replied.

In short order, we had our coffees and had picked up my grandmother. Once she was ensconced in the back seat and Alice was driving toward home, Gram asked, "Well, did you do the dirty yet?"

Alice had just taken a sip of her coffee and sputtered as she lowered it to the cupholder in the console between the seats. "Can you get me a napkin?" Alice asked, glancing at me. "There are some in the glove compartment."

I handed one over before glancing over my shoulder to Gram. "What the hell?" I asked, keeping my tone light.

My grandmother's eyes twinkled with mischief as she shrugged. "I like to stay up to speed. I missed the news while I was in the hospital."

"You've been in the hospital for one day," I countered with a roll of my eyes.

My grandmother shrugged, entirely unabashed. "A lot can happen in a day."

Chapter Twenty-Two

ALICE

"Do the dirty." I chuckled to myself as I finished cleaning the kitchen sink.

My cheeks got hot just thinking about Bea's comment. Jonah had rolled his eyes, handling it with more aplomb than I could have if she were my grandmother.

Honey nudged my hand with her nose when I turned away from the sink. Pausing, I knelt beside her, smoothing my palms down her cheeks, her favorite way to be petted.

"How are you doing, sweet girl?" I murmured.

Her tail swished through the air. I didn't know what mix she had in her, but one of them involved feathering along her legs and the back of her haunches and tail. She was turning out to be a very sweet girl. I straightened, asking, "Are you ready to go to the office?"

She did a little dance on her three legs. She loved going to the office. I knew I would have to cut back on the treats. She was still putting on weight from being so thin and undernourished, but she didn't have far to go before she achieved a healthy weight.

After a quick shower, I hurried out to the SUV and helped her get into the passenger seat, where I clipped on her security lead. She had quickly settled into a routine with me and liked sleeping on the dog bed in the hallway just outside my door. I had placed a bed at the foot of my bed, but she rarely used it, preferring to keep an eye on things.

Once we got up in the morning, I took her for a walk by the lake, playing fetch for a few minutes. For now, she still liked jumping into the lake and swimming, but it wouldn't be long before it would be too cold. Sometimes, I ate a quick breakfast at home, but now that I was going into town every day, I preferred to swing by Firehouse Café. Janet's coffee was better than anything I could make at home, and I loved getting something for breakfast there. More than the coffee and food, I savored being home again and seeing people I'd known for many years. It felt like I was slipping back into the routine of belonging somewhere.

A short drive later, I parked outside of Firehouse Café. I cracked the passenger side window enough for Honey to poke her head out if she wanted. "I'll be back in a few minutes," I assured her.

Her tail swished against the seat, and she leaned over to lick the back of my hand as I reached for my key fob, where it rested in the cupholder. Moments later, I was at the front of the line, and Janet was cocking her head to the side. "I think I have your coffee memorized. An Americano with a dash of cream?"

I grinned. "You got it. I have no idea how you remember everybody's coffee."

Janet shrugged. "I only remember the regulars. They have to come more than once a week unless they've been coming for years, or they get something really basic," she explained with a chuckle. She began preparing my coffee. "Anything to eat?"

"I'll take a bagel with smoked salmon cream cheese and maybe two egg bites." My gaze scanned the chalkboard menu.

"What kind of egg bites?"

"Oh, I have options?"

Janet tapped a button on the espresso machine, replying, "Of course. Vegetarian or not."

"I'm not a vegetarian."

She grinned. "Bacon and cheese is the meat option today."

"I'll take two."

She called out my order over the half door into the kitchen, turning to add, "I'm starting dog biscuits for you."

"Me?"

Janet nodded. "Yes. Dog-appropriate snacks. I can't believe I haven't done it before." She gestured to the display case. Tucked into the corner were dog-shaped biscuits.

I burst out laughing. "Well, I'll take two of those. Did you make them yourself?"

She nodded, looking satisfied with herself. "You told me what was safe. Every time you come in, you get a biscuit or something for her, but you always get the plain ones, so..." Janet shrugged as her words trailed off.

"I love it. I bet they'll be popular."

She fetched two of the biscuits for me, putting them in a paper bag and handing it over. While I was paying, she commented, "So you and Jonah?"

I felt the heat rise in my cheeks and tried to play it cool. "I'm sorry, what?"

Janet grinned, her eyes twinkling as she handed over my change and my coffee. "Bea thinks you two have a thing. She's sure of it. She said she caught you kissing."

Ah, the downsides to that sense of belonging and being back home—gossip, rumors, and speculation. The fact was Bea *had* seen us kissing. Even though we hadn't fessed up to doing the dirty when she had asked, I knew she wasn't stupid.

I sighed. "Maybe we were kissing. But it's no big thing."

"Why not? Jonah is a really great guy. And he's a hotshot firefighter now. He's totally sexy," Janet said, waggling her eyebrows.

I sputtered on the swallow of coffee I had just taken. Without missing a beat, Janet handed over a napkin.

I dabbed at the corners of my mouth and slid the napkin around the lid of my coffee to wipe off the mess. "It's really nice being back in town," I offered, choosing to ignore her last comment.

"Mm-hmm," Janet teased.

I glanced behind me, noticing no one else had arrived in line. I decided to take advantage of this little moment. "Did you know he was in a school shooting?" I asked, keeping my voice low.

She nodded, her gaze sobering immediately. "I did. He was on track to start teaching in college after finishing his PhD, but he decided not to."

My heart ached for a moment, remembering the careful look in his eyes when he'd explained the scars on his side.

"Bea says he doesn't talk about it," Janet added.

"His parents are coming up, you know to be close to Bea while she's still here. They worry about him."

"What happened is awful," I said, thinking the word "awful" was inadequate.

"Of course, it is," Janet agreed. "And it happens all the time. Whatever happens with you two, you be good to him. He needs someone to love him, and I know you would never hurt him."

My eyes widened. "How did we go from kissing to love?"

Janet shrugged. "I'm just sayin'. I think you'd be good for each other."

The bell chimed on the door to the café, and I glanced back to see Jonah walking in. My body reacted instantly. My heart beat faster as if clapping in joy at his mere presence. My belly felt all fluttery, and heat danced through my system, with little sparks scattering everywhere.

When I glanced back at Janet, her eyes held a knowing glint. I bit my lip, willing the heat rising in my cheeks to cool.

Chapter Twenty-Three

JONAH

Two weekends later

I hesitated. "Uh, well, I guess so," I finally said.

"We didn't really think this through," my mother said.

I had just picked my parents up at the airport. Apparently, they were under the impression they were staying where I was staying, which only had one bedroom.

"I'll crash on the couch tonight and figure something out," I offered.

My mother leaned forward from the back seat, squeezing my shoulder lightly. My father glanced over from the passenger seat, adding, "We can figure something out too." My mother insisted on riding in the back so my father had more leg room. "So how is she?" he asked.

"Gram seems okay. She had a scare, mostly feeling weak and dehydrated from what I understand."

"That's not like her," my father replied.

"I don't think she has much of an appetite," I explained. "Her spirits are good, though."

My mother let out a soft sigh behind me. "It's just hard to believe she may only have a few more months."

"I know. She's as nosy as ever, though," I offered with a chuckle. "I know you're worried, and so am I, of course. I think you'll feel better when you see her."

"I hope so. How are you?" my mother asked.

I caught her eyes in the rearview mirror before looking back toward the road. "Pretty good."

The space inside my truck felt loaded for a moment. I knew my parents wanted to ask if I was thinking about teaching again or if I was having nightmares and flashbacks. I didn't want to talk about it. Not with them.

I loved them both dearly and was grateful to have parents like them, but talking about the shooting and its aftermath with them was too much. I'd seen a therapist after it happened. All of us at the school had been automatically referred for an assessment. I still had the option to see the therapist I'd met for the first few months afterward. Since I'd moved, it had dwindled to a session every month or so over videoconference.

Knowing that they would only keep worrying if I didn't say something, I offered, "I'm sleeping well, and I love my job here."

"That's good to hear," my mother said with a forced cheerfulness in her tone.

Something that was rarely discussed when you experience an event that fell into the horrifying category was that those who cared about you and loved you had their own trauma and pain related to the event. It was like when someone lost someone they loved, and you were never sure how often you should check in with them, whether you should be more discreet about it, and so on. This was even bigger because that kind of loss was more common. People wondered, worried, and wanted to fix it for you and undo it. Yet you could never undo that. You couldn't unwind time.

My parents shifted to more mundane topics, with my father asking questions about Willow Brook, his hometown, and my mother sharing that they were considering retiring here.

A short while later, we were at my grandmother's house. She had made more brownies, calling over to me, "And I made a batch for Alice. You must take them over to her. Also, I checked with her, and you can have her spare bedroom."

"Excuse me?" I glanced over, my brows hitching up.

My grandmother had a gleam in her eyes. "There's no spare bedroom here, and your parents need a bed, so they'll stay in the cabin. Alice has a two-bedroom house, fully furnished. She said it was fine."

I had *so* many thoughts. I should've known my grandmother would do this. All I did was nod. I knew better than to let her see my reaction. "Okay."

"Alice?" my mother prompted as she turned to glance over from where she sat at the kitchen table.

Gram nodded. "Her parents lived next door. She moved back to town recently. Do you remember her from summer visits?"

"Oh yes, such a nice girl. What is she doing? I recall her parents died, but I don't know what happened."

I did not know this detail, so I listened as I filled a

mug of coffee from my grandmother's ever-full coffee pot.

"Oh, yes," my Gram said as she crossed over to the kitchen table, setting down a plate of brownies in the middle before seating herself across from my mother. "They died in a fishing accident. A storm came in while they were out, and the boat capsized. They never found the bodies. It was so sad."

My heart twisted sharply in my chest.

"What a terrible way to die," my mother said, her hands flying to her chest.

Gram nodded. "I know. Alice returned for the funeral, and I checked on the house while she was away. She was in veterinarian school at the time. She's taking over the vet clinic here." My grandmother looked over toward my father, who entered the room. "Do you remember the old vet, Dr. Dan?"

"Of course," my dad said. "Surely he's retired by now." He immediately walked across the kitchen and reached for a brownie.

Gram nodded. "If you ask me, he worked too long. He retired two years ago, and they've been covering the clinic with visiting vets. They're giving the business to Alice."

"Well, that's nice," my mother said. "She should be about your age."

My mother looked up at me. I stood beside my father, sipping my coffee and schooling my expression to be nonchalant. "Oh, yeah?"

My mother nodded. "Well, maybe a few years younger. You were always off doing your own thing when we visited in the summer."

My grandmother drummed her fingertips on the table. "Alice should be about three or four years younger than you. When you're younger, that seems like a big gap, but now hardly at all."

I didn't even look in my grandmother's direction as I reached for a brownie.

Chapter Twenty-Four

ALICE

Jonah: *Rumor has it my grandmother guilted you into letting me use one of your guest bedrooms.*

A little laugh slipped out as I read Jonah's text message. Bea didn't have to guilt me, but she would've. She was primed for it. I had mixed feelings about Jonah staying in my house for an undetermined time. Ever since our night together, I couldn't stop thinking about it. I was in an endless cycle of mental debate. My body thought spending as much time as possible with Jonah was a fantastic idea, while my mind thought it was a little risky.

I had never planned to come home and dive into a relationship. I figured romance was in the distance for me. I needed to settle back into my hometown and focus on getting my business up and running.

Yet Jonah was ridiculously tempting.

"Why are you staring at your phone and smiling?" Tiffany's voice reached me, and I turned to see her leaning in the doorway of the break room.

"No reason," I replied, aiming for my tone to sound casual.

"Now, you're blushing," she pointed out.

"I'm your boss. You're not supposed to grill me," I returned, my cheeks getting even hotter.

Unabashed, my only employee shrugged. "Maybe so, but—" She paused and cleared her throat. "Somebody texted you, and it's got you all hot and bothered. Also, you're not the controlling kind of boss. Willow Brook is the size of a freaking thimble. We have to be on good terms."

I lowered my phone, grinning over at her. "I'm not that kind of boss. It's Jonah."

Her grin widened. "Oh, Jonah, who totally has the hots for you? Jonah, who you *totally* have the hots for," she teased.

I twisted my lips to the side. "No matter who has the hots for who, I'm wading into a potentially complicated situation."

"What's up?" Tiffany pushed away from the door and sat down across from me.

We had just finished up for the day. I had waved goodbye to the family who had gotten a mini pig that was not a mini pig. She was big now, and her name was Petal. She was adorable and sweet, and the kids loved her, so the family had turned their garage and yard into a space where Petal could live.

Tiffany and I were working really well together. Everything meshed. I needed someone to take the reins from Georgia and Natalie and let me focus on the rest. Tiffany had done that effortlessly. She had initiative, and she was funny.

We had agreed to check in every morning so she could get me up to speed on any changes she was making and cover anything I needed to weigh in on opinion-wise. Otherwise, she had my schedule filled up already. I thought I could consider doing surgery once I found a vet assistant. I had already put some feelers out to a few of the vet practices in Anchorage. I needed someone to cover emergencies for me on occasion.

I leaned back in the chair across from her. "Bea called me." I felt my cheeks getting hot just thinking about it. "She said Jonah needs a place to stay."

"No, he doesn't," Tiffany said, her brows arching. "He's staying in her little B&B place. I think he's even paying rent."

"Oh, he has been," I confirmed, "But his parents are here to stay since Bea is sick, and we don't know how long she's going to be around here." Every time I thought about that, my heart hurt a little bit. "She doesn't have a big house, just one bedroom. It's her and Dennis, and they're—"

"Newlyweds," Tiffany interjected.

"Exactly. The B&B is also one bedroom. It just has a loft. Bea called me and said she didn't want Jonah to have to sleep on anybody's couch. I have plenty of space. It's a three-bedroom house, so I said yes. Because—"

"It's the neighborly thing to do," she offered with a saucy grin.

"It is. I just don't know if it's a smart idea."

"I think it's a *great* idea."

"Why do you say that?" I asked.

"You might as well enjoy the company," she said, biting her bottom lip to keep from bursting into laughter.

"I don't know if that's the best plan," I replied, feeling flustered as heat rose into my cheeks.

Tiffany shrugged. "You already said yes. Either figure out how to keep your hands off Jonah or put your hands all over Jonah." She gave up trying not to laugh and snickered, her eyes glinting with mischief.

"For someone who's sworn off romance, you're pretty positive this is a good idea."

I didn't know what happened, but Tiffany was all "no way, no how" as far as anything to do with love, romance, or dating for herself.

She shrugged. "We're not talking about me. We're talking about you and Jonah," she said with an airy wave. "You've already said yes, so he's obviously going to stay at your place. At this point, the problem is if he doesn't stay there, both of you are stuck wondering how you'll explain that. It'll just create more gossip."

Resting my elbows on the table, I dropped my face in my hands with a groan. I brushed my hair back as I lifted my head. "You're right."

She waggled her eyebrows. "So deal with it."

Chapter Twenty-Five

JONAH

Despite my misgivings, which were significant, I was going to stay at Alice's place. If I didn't, that would create more questions for my grandmother. Best to play it off as if it was no big deal.

Alice: *Text me when you get home, and I'll meet you at the parking area.*

Me: *No need. My knee is fine. I already got cleared to drive.*

I knew she thought I needed help with the groceries without her saying it.

A little while later, Honey tippy-tapped around my legs in the kitchen. I leaned over to greet her, stroking down her back and murmuring, "Hey there, girl."

"I've already spoiled her rotten," Alice said when I straightened.

"Isn't that the point of having a dog?" I quipped.

Her smile was wide. "I knew I liked you, Jonah." Her comment was light and teasing.

I sensed we both felt it at the same moment, that snap and crackle in the air between us.

I rested a hand on the counter, saying, "I'm sorry Gram put you on the spot."

Alice shrugged. "It's no worry. And it's really no problem for you to stay here. I definitely have more room than your grandmother and your parents."

She eyed me, resting her hands on her hips. "Plus, you know it'll be worse if you don't stay. Then she's going to wonder all about it."

I chuckled. "Exactly my thinking. Oh, I have brownies."

I crossed over to where I had left my backpack on the chair. Unzipping it, I pulled out two foil-wrapped brownie trays.

Alice grinned. "Well, we know what we're having for dessert. Do you want dinner?" she asked as she leaned over and opened a lower cabinet, coming out with a scoop of dog food that she promptly dumped into a bowl by the wall.

Honey gobbled up her food while I replied, "You don't need to cook for me every night."

"Jonah, we're friends. I like to cook for myself. You can cook for me another night. Let's not be weird."

"Don't you think it's weird that my grandmother's trying to set us up and forcing me on you?"

Alice shrugged. "No, it's par for the course for your grandmother. Now, I was planning to make homemade mac & cheese. I always crave that when it's getting cold. Does that sound good?"

"It sounds great. Just tell me how I can help."

With Alice directing me, we cooked. I discovered she liked to listen to the news, and then she switched over to podcasts, giving me a choice between current topics and comedy.

Once we put the tray of mac & cheese in the oven,

she immediately began cleaning up, trying to shoo me away from helping.

"Alice, I like a clean kitchen as much as you do," I said lightly. "Why don't you sit down and have that glass of wine you haven't even touched while I take care of this?"

She shrugged. "I'm used to living alone." She acquiesced and sat down, sipping the wine and filling me in on how things were going with her vet clinic.

I had everything put away in the dishwasher, the sink cleaned, and the counters wiped down inside of a few minutes. I joined her at the table.

Honey was sound asleep on a bed in the hallway. "Is that her favorite spot?" I asked, gesturing toward her.

"She loves it. At night, that's her favorite spot. In the daytime, she likes to be in the living room." Alice gestured to the couch. "She sits up there on the back of the couch and looks out the windows. Dog television."

I grinned. "She seems settled in with you."

Alice nodded. "She is. She loves it at the clinic too."

"Does she do okay with the other animals coming in and out?"

"She does. I wasn't sure how that part was going to go. We mostly keep her behind the reception desk or with me in the back when I'm between appointments. She's figured out she's not allowed in the exam rooms."

"Makes sense. That would probably be stressful for the other animals coming in."

"Exactly," Alice said.

Not much later, she showed me the guest room. She even had fresh towels for me on the dresser. "And you have your own bathroom," she said, pointing at one of the doors off to the side of the room.

"That's nice. I didn't expect that."

"It's a small one with one of those tiny stand-up showers, but it's all yours." She glanced at her watch. "I'm going to take Honey out and go to bed."

The chemistry between us was still sparking, as it did whenever I was around her. Even though we hadn't discussed it, it seemed we both realized it was wise to keep a little distance, especially if I was going to be here all the time.

I lay in bed not much later, listening to the shower running and trying not to think about Alice's pink and flushed skin from the shower the morning after our night together.

I told myself this was a smart move. My life was complicated enough. I didn't need to make things messy by getting too involved with Alice when I knew I couldn't give her what she deserved.

Chapter Twenty-Six

ALICE

I fell asleep, restless with my thoughts spinning around Jonah and the ever-present humming desire thrumming through my system. I finally fell asleep, only to wake shortly after midnight. A sound startled me out of my sleep, and I sat up quickly.

I glanced over to see Honey wasn't on her bed just outside the doorway, but I heard her claws clicking across the floor in front of the guest bedroom. I slipped out of bed, tiptoeing into the hallway and stopping in front of Jonah's door. I could hear motion and restless breathing, followed by a muffled shout and a cry.

I didn't even hesitate and opened the door, pushing through. The sheets were tangled around Jonah's waist, and he kicked a leg when he cried out again. I reached the edge of the bed, shaking his shoulder. "Jonah!" I whispered loudly.

His eyes flew open, and he stared at me blankly for a moment. His skin was damp with sweat.

"Alice?" He spoke slowly as he appeared to register who I was and where he was.

"You were having a nightmare," I said.

Honey had followed me into the room and rested her nose on the edge of the bed right by his hand. She nudged it and softly nuzzled her head against his hip.

He sat up, looking from me to Honey before he gave his head a little shake. "I suppose I did." His voice was slightly hoarse, the edges of his words ragged.

I reached to straighten the covers and realized the sheets were damp with sweat. My heart tumbled in my chest, twisting with a sharp ache.

"Just come to my room," I said before I could think better of it.

Jonah seemed dazed when I curled my hand around his. He swung his legs off the bed and followed me into my bedroom. Honey nudged his knee as we crossed the hallway, and he leaned down to stroke between her ears. She hopped on her bed, circling several times before laying down with a sigh as if she was satisfied everyone in her world was okay.

"Do you want to shower?" I heard myself asking, thinking his skin was cold and clammy.

He was wearing nothing but a pair of fitted boxer briefs. He looked at me for a moment and then nodded. I walked into the bathroom off my bedroom, reaching in to turn it on and testing the water. "It's hot," I said.

He shucked his boxers and stepped into the shower. I stood there for a minute, wondering what to do. Then I hurried across to the guest room, finding a clean pair of boxer briefs off the top of his opened backpack. I fetched a clean towel out of the closet in the hallway and returned to the bathroom. He was already stepping out of the shower, so I simply handed him the towel.

A sense of uncertainty slipped through me as I climbed into bed again. He was a grown man. It wasn't like he needed to come to bed with me after a nightmare, but the sheets in the guest room were damp.

A moment later, he slipped under the covers, rolling over to look at me as he rested on one elbow. "Are you sure about this?"

We looked at each other quietly in the dim light from the hallway.

"It's unpleasant to go back to damp sheets, and I only had one extra set," I pointed out.

"Ah." He paused, his gaze pensive. "Was I that loud?"

"It woke me up. And Honey." He nodded. I waited for a beat. "Do you remember your dream?" I heard myself asking, immediately wishing I could take back the question.

He was quiet for a long moment before he rolled onto his back, resting his arm behind his head and cushioning it on the bend of his elbow.

"It's the same nightmare every time. It's just the beginning of the shooting. The sound of the gunshots and the commotion and confusion. I think I remember getting shot, but that wasn't really the worst part."

"No?" I rolled onto my side, resting my palm on his chest.

"No. It was seeing the blood and the four kids who were shot right in front of me."

"I'm so sorry," I whispered.

He rolled his head to look at me. "Obviously, it's not your fault. I'm sorry too. We're all sorry. Every time there's a school shooting, we're all so sorry. Did you know guns are the most frequent cause of death for children in our country?"

"I could've guessed."

"We're failing," he said, his voice ragged on the edges as if the pain was tearing at his words.

"We are," I agreed.

He shifted, uncurling his arm from where it was tucked and rolling to face me. He brushed my hair back from my cheek, catching a curl in his fingers and spinning it around.

I could hear the echoing beat of my heart and the rush of blood in my ears as his eyes skated over my face. I slept in a soft fitted cotton tank top because I hated when fabric twisted around my body when I slept. His fingers slipped out of the curl and traced along the edge of my tank top.

Goose bumps prickled over the surface of my skin. I could feel the heat rising inside me, the need sharp.

"I like you, Alice. More than I should," he murmured. "This wasn't supposed to happen."

"I like you too, Jonah. More than I should." I could feel my lips curling at the corners. "This wasn't supposed to happen."

My voice was a raspy whisper as my pulse began to race. Butterflies took flight, tingling inside my belly and sending sparks scattering everywhere, lighting little bonfires.

Jonah's hand slipped down, his touch grazed over my breast, and my nipple tightened, almost begging for more. His palm slid down over my belly and up under the hem of my tank top. His touch was warm and sure, the subtly calloused surface of his palm sending a hot shock to my system. My belly tightened, and I bit my lip as he shifted closer, his lips dusting over mine. He nipped my bottom lip, tugging lightly.

I couldn't hold back the moan that escaped. He captured it with his mouth, instantly claiming mine in an overpowering, deep kiss. His thumb teased over my nipple before he cupped my breast fully. I arched into him, feeling my pussy clench. I gasped when his palm slipped down again, coasting over my belly and dipping between my thighs. He pressed his fingers over my clit through the thin fabric of my underwear, and my hips bucked into his touch.

I let out a whimper into our kiss at the last tease of his tongue against mine. He lifted his head, sucking in air. I was relieved to hear his breath was as ragged as mine. We stared at each other in the quiet darkness of my bedroom.

He pushed my tank top up, murmuring, "Let's get this off."

I rolled off the side of the bed, shimmying out of my underwear as he kicked his boxers free. I glanced down, curling my palm around his thick shaft. His cock pulsed under my touch, and I wiped my thumb over the tip, smearing the drop of pre-cum rolling out. I couldn't resist and leaned over, swirling my tongue around the tip.

Jonah groaned as I sucked him into my mouth. I savored the salty flavor dancing across my tongue as I swirled it around the tip once again. He fell back into the pillows, his hand tangling in my hair. "Fuck, Alice," he growled as I sucked him in again.

I teased him, bringing him into my mouth fully and savoring another drop of pre-cum when I released him. I lifted my head, a surge of power rolling through me when his eyes met mine. We stared at each other for a moment before he shifted up, saying, "I need to taste you, and I want to be inside you when I come."

Before I could argue the point, he moved quickly, rolling me onto my back. He paused. "I need to get a condom."

Without thinking, my hands gripped his sides. "Wait." He lifted a brow in question. "I'm on the pill. I trust you." I didn't want to think too hard about how much I wanted to feel him inside me without anything between us.

He was quiet, his eyes holding mine steadily. After a beat, he asked, "Are you sure about that?"

"About being on the pill?"

His lips twitched. "No."

"I trust you."

Intimacy shimmered between us. He took a quick breath before whispering, "Okay. I trust you too."

There was no more talking then. His hands splayed across my belly before he captured one of my tight, achy nipples with his mouth and sucked sharply, sending sensation sizzling through my system. I gasped, falling back into the pillows. He blazed a trail of hot kisses over my belly, each one a shock of sensation, spinning into all the sensations ricocheting through me.

One palm slid up the inside of my thigh, pushing my knee out to the side. I felt the stubble of his five o'clock shadow against my skin, the gentle and electrifying feel of his lips pressing a kiss on the acutely sensitive skin inside my thigh. I was dripping wet, clenching for him at my core. He licked into my folds, and I cried out sharply.

My fists were curled into the sheets, and my hips were rising to meet him as he sank two fingers inside me, knuckle deep, before drawing them out and plunging them in again as he teased me with his tongue.

I was near incoherent with need while he fucked me slowly with his fingers. My climax was rising swiftly. I felt drawn tight inside. The claws of pleasure sank more deeply until he finally sucked lightly on my clit as his fingers pumped into me once more. The piercing pleasure finally crested into a crashing wave, and I shuddered so hard my mind went blank.

He stayed with me. I slowly came to, the pleasure spinning through me in little eddies, like a tide rolling out after a big wave crashed to shore. His palms moved over my belly again, his eyes on me as he rose above me.

I was restless. I needed the feel of him filling me completely.

I felt the give of the mattress as his knee pressed between my thighs. His weight came over me, and I felt the press of his crown notching at my entrance. He laced his fingers into mine, stretching my arms over my head. His eyes held mine, his gaze intent and intimate. I felt exposed, as if he had somehow unlocked a key to my heart and soul when I didn't even know there was a lock on it.

He held still until I rocked my hips restlessly against him. Inch by inch, he sheathed himself inside me until he was buried to the hilt. His speech bordered on slurred when he murmured, "Alice, you feel so good."

My breath came in sharp little pants. I nudged my hips against him and whispered in a husky rasp, "I need you."

Chapter Twenty-Seven

JONAH

I need you.

Alice voiced the feeling beating like a drum in my heart, body, and soul. I didn't know if it was because of the nightmare that had woken me, but I felt stripped raw, and my defenses burned to ash. Nothing but the smoldering ruins of my fierce need for Alice were left standing.

I held still, the silky clench of her rippling around me. Her skin was damp, and I could feel the tight peaks of her nipples pressing against my chest. Her fingers tightened around mine, and I drew back, sinking in again, tightening my grip around her hands as we settled into a rhythm. Her hips rose to meet every thrust of mine.

I stared into her eyes with nothing but the light of the moon as I watched her. Sensation overtook me. My release felt like lightning sizzling through my system. My balls tightened, and I could feel her climax threatening again with tremors rolling through her body. Her legs tightened around my hips as she murmured, "Jonah, now."

She arched against me, letting out a keening cry. I followed her over the edge instantly, my own release a fiery snap. I distantly heard myself calling her name just before I collapsed against her.

We shuddered together for a moment before I had enough sense to loosen my grip on her hands and roll over, holding her tight against me.

Alice rested against my chest as we breathed together. I could feel the drumming beat of her heart against mine. Her body softened when she tucked her head into my shoulder. My arms relaxed, and I sifted my fingers through her tousled curls.

I still felt raw, still exposed, still vulnerable. But for the first time since I'd been having those nightmares, which happened almost twice a week—not because I was keeping track—I had forgotten the nightmare. And I wasn't cold and restless, and I didn't need to wish I could slip into darkness.

Chapter Twenty-Eight

JONAH

The following morning, I woke to the sound of water running and the feel of a dog's cool nose nudging my hand. Opening my eyes, I rolled my head to the side and grinned at Honey. Her tail started wagging, her feet tapping on the floor as she wiggled and danced. There wasn't anything much better than waking up to that kind of pure joy.

I rolled up and swung my feet to the floor. Honey tucked her head against the mattress between my knees, and I scratched behind her ears, chuckling as her entire body wagged madly.

The sound of the shower stopped, and I stood from the bed. As I walked into the bathroom, Alice turned. Her cheeks were pink and flushed from the steam, and her curls wet. She had a towel wrapped around her, and I had to fight the urge to cross over and tug it off.

"Good morning," she said, her voice husky.

Honey had followed me in and began circling Alice's legs.

"Morning. Honey woke me up."

"She's a friendly alarm, isn't she?" Alice teased as she petted Honey.

"Definitely."

"I'll start some coffee," she said, slipping past me before my impulses could get the best of me.

As I showered, my thoughts spun back to the night before. It wasn't as if the memories were clear in retrospect. Instead, it was the sensations—sharp, intense, and evoking an intimacy even in recollection that I wanted to eschew from inside. And yet, I couldn't.

I wanted to tell myself to be smart about this. To find a way to keep my hands off Alice while I was staying here indefinitely. That wish was a tiny voice in the wind. The force of my need for her was too powerful. While the sense of exposure and raw intimacy was intimidating, I craved that as well.

A few minutes later, I was dressed and in the kitchen. Honey was perched on the back of the couch in the living room and looking out the window. Alice glanced over as she was filling a mug with coffee. "Here," she said, handing it over as I approached.

"This is mine?"

"Yes." She already had another mug waiting and filled that one, adding, "There's half and half in the fridge. I'm going by the store today. Why don't you text me some things you want?"

"How about I go? I mean, I'm staying here, and you're hosting me."

Alice shrugged as she turned and rested her hips against the counter. I fetched the half and half, pouring a dollop in my mug and handing it to her. After a swallow of coffee, she replied, "It's neither here nor there. I hate splitting hairs on things like groceries. We can take turns shopping. If you plan to have breakfast here, I've got some eggs and bagels, but that's it. I usually stop by Firehouse Café on my way into the clinic."

Just then, her house phone rang. We both swiveled to look at where it was mounted on the wall. It was one of those old phones, from the 80s probably. The sound of the ring was shrill in the kitchen.

Alice's eyes were wide when she looked at me. "I forgot about that phone. I didn't even know it was on. I haven't been paying for it. So weird."

It rang again. "Are you going to answer it?" I asked.

"I can't imagine who even has this number," she finally said.

The phone continued to ring. "I'll get it if you want."

She nodded. Crossing the kitchen, I lifted the phone. Honey leaped off the couch and trotted to my side, staring curiously at the phone.

"Hello?"

"Hi, I'm calling for Alice," a man said.

I couldn't say why, but a sense of trepidation slithered down my spine. I looked over at Alice, moving the phone away and mouthing, "It's for you."

She shook her head quickly, her damp curls swinging with the motion.

"I'm sorry, there's no one here by that name," I said into the receiver. "May I ask who's calling?"

"I don't know who you are," the man said, his tone carrying a whiff of threat. "But I know Alice lives there. Tell her Tyler Black called."

I simply hung up the phone. I took a swallow of coffee as I turned to face her. "Who the hell is Tyler Black?"

Alice's face turned ashen. "Oh god," she muttered.

"Hey, are you okay?" I crossed over to her, stopping by the counter and resting my hand on it beside her.

She took a deep breath, letting it out with a sigh before she took a gulp of her coffee. When she lowered her mug, she looked over at me. "He's the guy who chased me out of my last job."

"Uh, okay," I said slowly. "Why the hell is he calling you, and how would he even get this number?"

She shrugged. "Seeing as I didn't even know the phone was on, I have no idea. I'm assuming it's still listed under my parents' name. I'll have to get it turned off."

"Why would he be calling?"

"When I was in vet school, I interned at a local clinic and then took a job there. It's a large clinic. They did pretty well, but they started to have problems with accounting. Because I helped with data entry, I figured out it was the son of one of the owners. Not a vet, but the person who handled the business end of things. He figured out that I figured it out, and I ended up leaving because it wasn't worth dealing with him."

"He accused you of something?"

Alice shook her head quickly. "No. He was siphoning money and creating problems with one of the main suppliers. Technically, he didn't get me fired, but he made it very uncomfortable for me to stay. I ended up having a conversation with the owners about it. When this job came up, I decided to just cut my losses and come here. HR didn't seem to care when I told them what I found. It wasn't a secret where I was going, so maybe that's how he found me."

"Alice, I think you should just turn everything over and make a police report." I sensed massive gaps in the information, but my gut told me something bad was happening here.

Alice let out another sigh, worry chasing through

her eyes. "But then it's a whole thing." She bit her bottom lip, worrying it.

"Is there more to this?" I finally asked.

She took a deep breath, letting it out in a gust. "Unbeknownst to me, he took a photo of me in the locker room at the clinic and threatened me with it."

Fury rose inside, hot and turning icy cold. "Alice, are you serious?"

Her cheeks went pink. She swallowed as she nodded. "Yeah."

"Alice, he should be charged for that."

She lifted a hand, letting it fall. "I don't want to go through all of it. It's not worth it. I cut my losses and left. I made sure that HR knew about the photo, and they told me they would address it, but they didn't seem that concerned. I don't know what they did, if anything, in response."

All I wanted was to comfort her. I set my mug down and turned to face her, wrapping my arms around her. She tucked her head into my chest, and I could feel her taking slow deep breaths. I moved my hand up and down her back in a soothing pass.

After a moment, she lifted her head, peering up at me. "He's just an asshole."

"I learned something when I worked as a teacher."

"What?"

"HR departments are fine, and they have a place. But they're mostly there to protect the place they work for. When someone commits a crime, you can report it to HR, but you should also report it to the police. When I was a teacher, things happened all the time. Say a kid would literally assault someone or be sexually inappropriate. The school handled it internally. Even when they were acting with good intentions, they were always trying to take care of both sides and treat them as equals in the situation, and doing their best to make sure no one filed a complaint against the school. When it comes to minor stuff, whatever. But when it comes to crimes, like someone taking a picture of you changing somewhere in a public place and using it to threaten you, you should report it to HR and the police. When you have information that someone is basically embezzling money, you should report it to HR and the police. For all you know, they ran it up the chain, but the chain is covering it up. I don't know why this guy's calling you, but take it out of his hands."

Alice studied me, uncertainty flickering in her gaze. "I hear you, but with his father being one of the owners, I don't think they wanted to make waves."

"Probably not. But the police don't care about that. I'll help you," I added.

Chapter Twenty-Nine

ALICE

I'll help you.

Jonah's words replayed in my thoughts. Just thinking about everything that went down with Tyler made my skin crawl, and I felt a little sick. The whole thing had been exhausting. Even more so, I'd felt so disappointed at how nothing happened when I told HR. I'd felt powerless to handle the situation.

I also couldn't help but keep wondering why Tyler called. Jonah's offer to help left me feeling unsure. I wasn't used to relying on anyone.

I was snapped out of my train of thought when Tiffany called, "Your appointment is here," into the intercom.

I hurried out of the break room into one of the exam rooms. A moment later, Tiffany was escorting them in the back. "Here," she said with a smile, "this is Pamela."

A cute little potbelly pig looked up at me. She was mostly black with a white spot on one side. She imme-diately approached me, nudging my knees with her snout. I couldn't help but smile as I looked down at her. "Well, hello, Pamela."

I looked up at the owner, a mother about my age, and her young child, who I guessed to be about five-ish. "Pamela doesn't feel good," the little girl announced as she stopped beside Pamela and put her hand on the pig's back.

"Well, let's take a look," I said.

A short while later, I had determined that Pamela had a bad case of indigestion. "Do you know if she got into anything?" I asked.

"It's always a possibility," Whitney, the mother, replied.

I sent them off with some diet recommendations, some medication to help settle Pamela's stomach, and scheduled Pamela's annual appointment. Tiffany was already there when I walked into the break room to grab lunch. She insisted we have a scheduled lunchtime, which I thought was amusing, but I appreciated it.

She looked up, announcing, "I went to Firehouse Café. We have sandwiches and fresh coffee. I got you some chai tea too."

Once seated, Tiffany remembered to dash to the front and lock the door. When she returned, she said, "Break time is sacred."

I snorted on the sip of my chai tea. I was really happy I'd hired her.

She sat down with a flourish, opening the bag from Firehouse Café and taking out two paper-wrapped sandwiches. "I got your favorite." She passed one across the table.

"How do you know I have a favorite?"

"Because you usually get the turkey with pesto and mozzarella."

I grinned over at her as I began unwrapping the sandwich. "You're right. I hadn't considered it officially a favorite, but..." I shrugged. "I suppose it is."

"So you're looking very rested today," she offered a moment later.

I finished a bite of my sandwich, willing my cheeks not to get red from the heat rising under the surface. "I slept well last night."

Tiffany waggled her eyebrows. "Jonah's staying with you now." She pursed her lips as she cast me a sly look.

My cheeks were on fire. I might as well give it up. "I surrender. I had awesome sex with Jonah last night." While I hadn't forgotten how his nightmare had woken me, those worries had been overshadowed by our encounter.

She bit her lip, looking way too smug. "Excellent."

"How is this excellent? This could get complicated." That wasn't even the half of it. "I don't know how long his parents will be here because—"

At my abrupt pause, Tiffany's gaze sobered. "Because we're all basically waiting for Bea to move to another plane," she said carefully.

"Is that what we're calling it?"

"Sure. I believe there's something other than what's here. It's not just plain old death."

I took a breath, letting it out as the sadness washed through me. "I've always loved Bea. She babysat me a lot. I'll miss her when she's gone, and I think Jonah will be devastated."

"Maybe. But this is definitely a cross-that-bridge-when-you-come-to-it moment. My point is we don't know how long Bea will be here. Maybe she'll surprise us all. That's always a possibility."

"I feel like I have to be realistic."

"I have noticed that you can be relentlessly realistic. It's possible you could call it pessimistic," Tiffany said, her tone dry as tinder.

I rolled my eyes. "Anyway, my point is Jonah will be my neighbor for the foreseeable future regardless of how long his parents are here."

"Do you know what his plan is?"

"What plan?" I started to panic inside.

"Bea is incredibly practical, more realistic than you probably. I'm sure she's already discussed with him whether she'll leave that B&B or her house to him. I got the info that Dennis is just staying with her for the time being. He has another house. But she wanted to stay by the lake. He doesn't intend to stay there after she passes."

"How do you know all this?" I shook my head slowly, almost amazed at Tiffany's ability to scope out information.

She chuckled. "My father. He's a terrible gossip. He and his buddies have been having a card game for years. They get together twice a month, I think. They know everything, and he tells me everything. I didn't have a nosy mom, but I have a nosy dad."

"I guess if I need to know something, I should ask you."

Tiffany finished chewing a bite of her sandwich, swallowing and replying, "Absolutely. I'll ask my dad if he hasn't already told me," she deadpanned.

"Back to Jonah, maybe I slept well, but it could get complicated. If it gets weird, he'll be next door." I lifted my hands in the air, letting them fall to the table. After a flustered sigh, I took an aggressive bite of my sandwich, chewing my feelings away.

"Was it good?" she teased a moment later.

My face got even hotter. I rolled my eyes. "Of

course, it was good." I took a swallow of tea. "I have a question."

"Ask away." She waved a hand airily.

I quickly filled her in on the situation at my last job and how Tyler called out of the blue this morning.

"What an asshole!" She narrowed her eyes, slapping her palm to the table in emphasis.

"Agreed. Jonah thinks since HR didn't do anything with the information, I should report it to the police."

"On board with that plan," she replied swiftly.

"Didn't you say you worked in HR at your last job?"

"I sure did. Not to say that the people who work in HR are not trying to be helpful and aren't good people, but Jonah's right. They're trying to follow the law, but they're also trying to protect the company. They won't tell you to file a police report because that's up to you. Sexual harassment gets reported to HR all the time. Not only did that ass take an illegal photo but he's also threatening to use it like revenge porn. Except you weren't even in a relationship with him."

I felt unsettled inside. Twisting my lips to the side, I nodded. "I think you're right. I suppose I just had faith they would handle it, but he's still working there."

"Please tell me you blind CC'd yourself on everything, so you have any of the emails related to this."

"I did do that. My friend who knew about it told me I should do that, so I did."

"I will sit right here with you while you call to report everything," Tiffany said firmly.

"Now?" Anxiety spun in my belly. "What if—" I began.

"Hon, your what-if is already hanging out there in

the universe. For all you know, that Tyler guy has already done something with that photo. Please tell me it was a shitty photo."

"It's not great, but I'm close to naked. I was changing after a surgery in the women's locker room. He had a camera installed in there." I paused, summoning my composure. "Okay," I said, to myself as much to her. "When's my next appointment?"

She smiled prettily. "Remember? We were going to take an extra half an hour at lunch today to go over the new calendaring system I set up. We can do that tomorrow. I can handle it, so let's take that time now to call."

Tiffany sat with me through both reports. It started with the police, who then routed me to the district attorney's office. It took a little longer than half an hour, but my next appointment was conveniently running late, and had texted Tiffany to let us know.

When I finished the second call and we tapped to end it, I looked at her. I was cold and clammy all over. "I can't believe I did that."

"You don't know what will happen now, but he'll probably be held accountable somehow. Fucking asshole," she announced, dipping her chin as if in emphasis.

"What if nothing happens?" I was instantly afraid it was all going nowhere.

Tiffany reached over, curling both of her hands around mine. "The detective told you they can't make any promises, but you have a paper trail for both situations. That cybercrime guy will reach out to the person who handles financial crimes, and they will follow up with you some more. While you don't know what will happen, if he dares to leak that photo now, he's fucked."

I took a shaky breath. Adrenaline was pumping through my system, and I was relieved and energized at the same time. We heard the bell chime, indicating someone had entered the waiting area.

Tiffany leaped up. "Get ready for—" She lifted the clipboard resting on the table. She said she liked to jot down the daily schedule because physically writing it was helpful for her. "Baxter," she announced, looking up with a grin. "Apparently, he's an elderly dog and very sweet."

Laying down by my feet the entire time, Honey sat up, wagging her tail and looking at me expectantly. I stroked my hands down over her ears and rested my forehead against hers for a moment. She licked my cheek and then stood to go curl up on her bed in the break room. She had fallen into her own schedule here. She liked to spend the mornings in the reception area under Tiffany's desk, occasionally checking on me between appointments. In the afternoon, she liked to hang out in the break room.

I was relieved I had a busy afternoon. As I drove home, I realized I had completely forgotten to go to the grocery store. I tapped my dashboard to call Jonah.

He picked up immediately. "Hey, what's up?"

At the mere sound of his voice, low with that subtle rasp, flutters spun in my belly, and my pulse started to race.

"Hey, I just realized I forgot to go to the grocery store, and I'm tired. What do you think about pizza for dinner?"

"You must've read my mind," he teased. "I'm actually at the pizza place right now. I figured even if you went to the store, I forgot to text you about it. I'm getting enough for both of us. They've got a pepperoni ready to go and mushroom. What's your preference?"

"Get both. I love both, and I love leftover pizza."

He chuckled, the sound spinning into the sensations already humming through my body. "You think like me. Need anything else? They've got breadsticks and some kind of dessert pizza."

"Dessert pizza sounds weird, but I'll take some breadsticks."

"Got it. I'll see you in a bit."

Chapter Thirty

JONAH

A week passed by. I was staying with Alice, ostensibly as her roommate, but in her bed every night. We couldn't get enough of each other.

She told me that she had filed a report with the police about that guy. Nothing had happened since. I sensed Alice was anxious.

We were going over to my grandmother's house for dinner tonight. Not an official date, but my grandmother had insisted that we both come. I wasn't ready for her or my parents to catch wind of what was happening with Alice and me. I supposed that was because I didn't know how to define it myself. Alice was rapidly unraveling the defenses around my heart. She was doing what I'd believed impossible.

Every time I thought too hard about it, uncertainty slid through me, just like now. I turned the radio up, ordering myself not to dwell on Alice. There was no need to define what we were.

Except I wanted to define it. That was the most terrifying part.

I parked beside Alice's SUV, climbed out, and

walked down the path that led to her house. My knee was fully healed up, and I was back at work. We hadn't gotten called out to another fire in the backcountry yet. With winter close, fire season was winding down. Work, for now, consisted of checking in at the station on a rotating schedule, working out, doing training exercises, and helping out with any local calls on occasion. Here and there, I still felt like my knee was a little looser than it had been before, but Charlie told me it would probably feel like that for a while and had given me some exercises to strengthen it.

When the trees opened up to a clearing with Alice's house just ahead, I saw Honey sniffing along the edge of the field. She lifted her head when my footsteps crunched on the leaves and dashed in my direction. For a three-legged dog, she was speedy.

I knelt beside her when she reached me, murmuring, "Hey, girl," as I stroked over her head and down her sides. I straightened, and she danced excitedly around me in a circle, walking at my side into the house.

I heard the shower running and knew exactly where I wanted to be.

I tossed Honey one of her favorite chew toys and stripped off my clothes in the bedroom in a hurry. I wanted to get in the shower before Alice was out.

"Hey there," I said as I walked into the bathroom.

"Hey," she replied, her voice muffled by the water.

"Mind if I join you?"

"Of course not."

I could see her silhouette through the glass door. Opening the door, my heart kicked faster, and I was instantly aroused. Alice's skin was rosy, and bubbles were rolling over her as she rinsed the shampoo out of her hair.

I stepped closer, leaning down to press a kiss to the side of her neck. She trembled slightly in my arms. "Hey," she repeated, her lips curving against my cheek as I wrapped my arms around her waist from behind.

"Hey, yourself," I murmured, continuing to make love to the side of her neck, well acquainted with how sensitive she was in that area.

I slid a palm up over her belly, gratified by the soap's slippery surface. I cupped her breasts with both palms, and her nipples tightened under my touch.

"Jonah," she whispered, although there wasn't a hint of protest in her voice.

"Mm-hmm?" I murmured against her neck as I lightly pinched her nipples.

"We have to go to your grandmother's," she whispered, the rasp of her voice barely audible over the sound of the water.

"We can make this quick."

I nipped her neck lightly before turning her around in my arms. With her cheeks pink, her hair slicked back, and her lips plump and full, I couldn't resist a kiss. Not that I could *ever* resist a kiss with Alice.

Her tongue twined sensually with mine, and I backed her up. I angled, turning and pressing her back against the tile. In another moment, I lifted her, hooking one knee high under my arm.

"Your knee," she protested.

I held her gaze, my lips kicking up into a grin as I replied, "My knee is officially fine. If my knee can handle fighting fires, it can handle this."

I filled her in a single swift surge. She rippled around me, her fingers pressing into the slick skin on my back.

Chapter Thirty-One

ALICE

My body still tingled from the aftershocks of the climax I'd experienced in the shower with Jonah. His fingers were laced with mine as we walked along the path from my house, past the small cabin where he had been staying, and then farther through the trees to his grandmother's house.

I caught myself stealing glances at him again and again. His eyes slid to meet mine one of those times. He stopped walking, turning to face me. "What?"

"Nothing. Just trying to, uh—" I paused, my cheeks getting hot. "I guess to make sure that I seem together." I swung a hand pointlessly in the air.

He smiled down at me. "You're always together, Alice."

"You just had your way with me in the shower, and now we're having dinner with your parents and your grandmother and her husband," I said pointedly.

"I could say *you* had your way with me in the shower," he teased lightly, squeezing my hand.

I rolled my eyes. "Talking about it isn't helpful."

He chuckled, and we began walking again. When

the trees opened up to the lawn beside his grandmother's house, in silent agreement, our hands had dropped away from each other once we stepped out of the trees. I knew his grandmother had plenty of suspicions about us, but she didn't need to see us holding hands. That would turn the flames of gossip into a full-on brushfire, fast and hard to control.

A few moments later, Bea was tugging me into a hug. She smelled like powder and flowers. As I hugged her back, I noticed she felt fragile in my arms, and my heart twisted.

"I think you saw them at the wedding," she said as she stepped back, "but these are Jonah's parents, John and Debbie."

I smiled at them. "We chatted at your wedding."

His mother waved. "Nice to see you again. Jonah is staying with you since we, well—"

"Kicked me out," he interjected dryly.

Debbie shrugged, casting him an apologetic look before she turned back to me and gave me a quick hug. "I was just talking to John, and we saw you on occasion when we visited in the summers. The last time I think you were in high school."

I nodded politely. "I'm sure. By then, I always had something going on."

"Isn't that the way of high school?" Jonah's father offered with a chuckle as he smiled over at me from where he sat at the kitchen table.

Bea had a kitchen with windows facing the lake and a large oval-shaped table beside them.

"Have a seat," Bea said, herding me toward the table and ordering Jonah to sit beside me. "We have assigned seats," she explained.

"We do?" Jonah countered with a grin.

Dennis appeared, smiling amongst the group, and

replied to Jonah's comment with, "You know your Gram. She likes things the way she likes things."

"Do you need any help with dinner?" I asked.

"Absolutely not," Bea said firmly.

A few minutes later, a large bowl of tossed salad was in the center of the table with two casserole pans, one of them Bea's salmon pie that she assured me had been one of my favorites when I was little, and another with scalloped potatoes with leeks, mushrooms, and chicken.

"Oh, now I remember the salmon pie!" I exclaimed after taking the first bite. "I'd love to have the recipe."

Bea looked over at Jonah's mother. "Can you please email it to her?" Her gaze shifted to me. "I don't email much, but Debbie has all my recipes."

"I'll make sure to jot down my email address before I go tonight," I offered with a smile.

I was acutely aware of Jonah's presence beside me —because my body was still reverberating with sensations from our encounter. That said, my manners kept me focused.

Dinner was relaxed, and I was glad we were there. It was hard not to think about why we were all there. Bea's energy was flagging, but she could still laugh and enjoy dinner.

I thought perhaps Jonah and I would skate through the evening without her putting us on the spot about anything. I should've known better. She waited until we let down our guard. Dennis insisted on cleaning up, shooing everyone else away, as he picked up the plates and began tidying up.

It was then Bea glanced over, commenting as she looked from Jonah to me and over to his parents, "Well, I'm sure you've heard."

John looked at her, his gaze was skeptical. "Heard what, Mom?"

She swung her hand airily toward Jonah and me. "Alice and Jonah." She leaned forward as I felt the blush burning up my cheeks. "They have a thing."

"We do not—" I began to sputter.

I felt Jonah's hands slide onto my knee under the table. He squeezed gently. "Don't give her any ammunition," he said lightly.

Jonah's father was unperturbed and simply shrugged while his mother eyed me with speculation in her gaze. "Mom loves to put people on the spot," John offered.

Bea grinned at this, offering, "I do." She looked at Jonah, waggling her eyebrows. "You should get things all settled before I go."

Jonah's head fell forward, his shoulders shaking as he laughed. When he lifted his head, he simply shrugged. "Gram, I love you."

Later that night, after we were back at my house with Honey curled up on the couch beside me and Jonah on my other side, I peered up at him. "We should've known she was going to do that."

He chuckled. "I knew she would say something. I just didn't know what or when. She never lets an opportunity pass."

I laughed softly. "I suppose you're right. I was worried, but when we got toward the end, I thought we might be in the clear."

"What will you tell your parents?" I couldn't help but ask.

Chapter Thirty-Two

JONAH

As I lay in bed beside Alice a week later, I pondered her question. I had answered her, but I hadn't *really* answered. I'd simply shrugged and assured her my parents weren't too nosy.

Alice's question got me thinking. I'd played it off like it was no big deal. Yet inside, my panic was building. She was starting to matter. Even though she knew about the shooting and my injuries, I didn't think anyone could understand how it had broken something in me.

Oh, I could go through the motions of life. I loved my parents, and I loved my grandmother. Still, the idea of falling in love with someone elicited trepidation and near terror if I allowed myself to dwell. Obviously, as a teacher, we attended plenty of meetings and trainings on how to respond in a potential shooter situation, which was fucking insane. Shootings were *that* common in our country. It was hard not to realize we simply didn't care enough to change anything. There was no sense in glossing it over.

But still, when that was your job, you could only do

it if you somehow tricked your brain into thinking it probably wouldn't happen to you. It wasn't me that I was worried about. It was the kids who died in front of me. It was Tina who got shot before the guy made it to the hallways. It was anyone who life could steal away in mere seconds of brutal, shocking violence.

That shooting stole so much faith I'd once had in the universe, a faith that you didn't ponder much until it was taken away. It was like with people. It could be easy to trust someone until they showed you otherwise. Trying to earn back trust was so much harder. The universe needed to regain my trust and faith, and I wasn't sure that was possible.

I didn't believe I could be the kind of man Alice deserved.

Alice was everything I could want. She was smart with a low-key but sly sense of humor, she was kind, she loved animals, she was down to earth, and she was *so* fucking sexy and sensual it took my breath away.

If I let her believe in me, she'd realize there was a dark corner of my heart, charred and burned, scarred as badly as the scars on my side where I'd been shot. She might lose faith in me when I didn't believe the universe could let me love someone. Because, fuck, the universe could break your heart harder than anything. The vagaries of chance were cruel and fickle.

I slept restlessly that night, waking when I heard Alice's voice. It sounded as if she was miles away. I struggled to break through the confusing haze of my nightmare. My heart was pounding, and my consciousness finally broke through. I was in Alice's bed, and she was right there. Her hand was on my shoulder as she gently shook me.

My skin was wet and clammy, and the sheets were damp. I felt sick as I dragged my eyes open. Her worried gaze met mine. After my recent nightmare, she'd put a night light in the room when I told her it helped to have a little light.

There was just enough light on my side of the bed — because she made sure to put it there — that I could see her eyes, the worry flickering in them, and the furrow between her brows.

Her hand was still on my shoulder, and she lifted it, smoothing my hair back where it was damp against my forehead. I knew she wanted to ask me if I was okay, but she didn't. That broke my heart. Because she knew I *wasn't* okay, so her question was unnecessary. It was as if she could see right through me. The blackness along the edges of my thoughts receded. I curled my fingers over the edge of the mattress, gripping it as a way to bring myself back into my body, into this moment.

"Let's get you in the shower," she said gently.

She climbed out of bed, rounding it on light feet and reaching for my hands to help me up. I let her lead me into the bathroom, stripping out of my boxers while she started the shower.

"There, it's hot." She herded me in and didn't follow me.

She knew I liked to shower alone when I was like this. This was the fourth time I'd had a nightmare while staying with her. There was a pattern to it now.

She would change the sheets on the bed while I showered. They would be dry and cool when I returned. I didn't deserve her. Oh, I could go through the motions of everything she did. But my heart didn't have the depth and breadth hers did. I couldn't handle loving someone and knowing the possibilities that life could throw her way.

Chapter Thirty-Three

ALICE

I slipped out of bed, careful not to wake Jonah. It was the weekend, and I knew he didn't have to go to the station. Moments later, I took a quick shower and changed into fleece leggings with a tank top and a flannel shirt. I tiptoed out of the bedroom and closed the door behind me. Honey was waiting for me on her bed in the hallway by our bedroom door.

Our bedroom door.

I brushed that thought away. I didn't need to be thinking of it like that.

Honey and I walked outside. Like most dogs, she was a creature of routine. She liked to dash down to the lake. Over the past few days, she stopped going into the water. It was cold and getting colder. This morning, hoarfrost was all over everything, glittering as the sun rays crested above the mountains and melted the frost. After Honey checked out the lakeshore, she did her business over along the edge of the trees, an area we didn't frequent. It was as if she wanted to be polite. Even then, I followed her and picked it up. There was no need to let dog poop pile up.

After I fed Honey, she liked to sit on the back of the couch and survey the yard. She seemed content to do that for hours. Some mornings, Jonah would be up, but I didn't expect him up just yet. The few times he had nightmares, he usually slept a full hour later. I imagined his psyche was exhausted from it. I always hesitated to ask more about the shooting. I didn't need to know more to realize it was a painful topic.

I settled in to work on my laptop, perusing an email Tiffany had sent and plunking around in the new payroll system she had set up. For now, it was just her and me in there, but she assured me we would be hiring a vet tech soon and potentially another veterinarian. I knew I needed to consider officially making her a manager. I planned to chat with Georgia and Natalie about the budgeting plans.

I took a swallow of my coffee just as my cell phone rang. Glancing down, I saw it was a number with a North Carolina area code.

I lifted it, sliding my thumb across the screen. "Hello?"

"Alice Hall, please," a man said.

"This is Alice."

"Alice, I thought I recognized your voice. This is Don Williams from the DA's office in Raleigh. I wanted to call and notify you that we're filing charges today against Tyler Black."

A sense of relief rushed through me, followed by anxiety tightening my chest. The feelings were tangled up together.

"Um, okay. What does that mean for me?"

"We're hoping we will not have to rely on your testimony if he chooses not to plead. We have plenty of evidence with the texts, emails, and photographs. We're still in the process of coordinating with the clinic regarding the financial charges. As I'm sure you're aware, it's complicated because his father is one of the owners. However, the other owners are cooperating and would like to proceed with charges. We'll keep you posted. Everything you've turned over has been very helpful in both situations."

He paused, and I took a shaky breath. "Is Tyler aware of the investigations?"

"We notified him this morning and issued a warning regarding any release of the photographs. You may have guessed, but yours are not the only photographs."

"How many are there?" I couldn't help but ask.

"It's a large clinic, and he had cameras hidden in the locker room. At this point, we have over eleven victims who have come forward. He's been blackmailing all of them. You seem to be the first he targeted. He moved on to blackmail the others."

"Oh my god," I breathed.

"As we've already requested, please notify us immediately if he tries to contact you in any way."

"Absolutely. So what do I do now?"

"We will keep you updated on the progress of both cases. I'm hopeful we can negotiate a plea deal that results in genuine consequences for him. If not, I believe our chances at trial are good, given our evidence. We have a strong case."

"Thank you for letting me know."

"Thank you for reaching out to us and reporting the crimes. People like this often get away with it solely because no one reports it out of fear. We're in contact with the team handling the investigation for the financial case. They will keep you updated. If you don't hear from them soon, I'll let you know any updates I have."

His words reminded me of precisely why I'd waited. We said our goodbyes. I lowered the phone and set it down on the counter. I couldn't believe something was actually happening. I still felt strange inside, unsettled and anxious. I didn't trust Tyler to take this news well. I'd seen his temper in action.

Only moments later, my cell phone rang again. When I saw another unknown number but with the same area code, I answered, thinking it was someone else in the DA's office. Mistake.

"Alice!" Tyler frantically barked in my ear, his tone menacing.

I almost jumped back at the sound, my hand clenching around the phone. Just then, I heard my bedroom door open and glanced down the hallway to see Jonah.

As if she sensed my tension, Honey leaped off the back of the couch, walking into the kitchen. Distracted, I said, "You're not supposed to contact me." My voice came out shaky.

Jonah walked into the kitchen just then, his alert gaze coasting over my face.

"It doesn't fucking matter if I'm not supposed to call you. Now that you've contacted the DA's office, I will make sure you regret it."

"You can't —"

Jonah's eyes narrowed as he crossed over to me. He paused, mouthing a question, "Can I take that?" As soon as I nodded, he swiftly reached for the phone, lifting it and saying, "Don't fucking call her."

Without another word, he lowered the phone, his thumb sliding across the screen to end the call. He looked furious but also almost scared. "Why the hell did you answer that call?" he demanded.

"Jonah, are you okay?" I asked as he turned, running his hands through his hair and walking over to stare out the windows.

He spun around, his eyes meeting mine briefly. "I have to go."

Before I could even react, he grabbed his jacket, stepped into his boots, and walked out the door.

Chapter Thirty-Four

JONAH

"You okay?" Graham asked.

After a punishing workout at the station and showering and changing, I had just walked into the kitchen and was pouring myself a cup of coffee. Glancing toward Graham where he sat at the kitchen table, I shrugged. "Fine. Why do you ask?" I crossed to the table, sitting down across from him.

"Uh, because you don't look fine," Graham offered.

Graham was more perceptive than I preferred at this particular moment.

"What gives?" he pressed.

I took a gulp of coffee, needing the bracing bitterness. I met his gaze, deciding honesty was my best approach. "I've kind of been seeing Alice, but not really."

"Uh, okay. Did you two have a fight or something?"

After another swallow of coffee, I lowered the mug to the table, tracing my thumb along the handle. "Not really. She's got this thing going on with this guy who threatened her back at her old job. It's complicated, and that's not even the point. Anyway, I fucking lost my shit and took the phone from her this morning when he called and told him to fuck off."

"Well, that makes sense," Graham said calmly. "All details aside, if somebody's threatening a friend, I'd tell them to fuck right off."

I cocked my head to the side. "Agreed, but it wasn't that. It's just how angry I was. Before the shooting, I was an easygoing guy. Since then, it's either I keep everything buttoned down or I feel like I'm about to explode."

"Ahhh," Graham said slowly. "I get it. Makes sense."

"It does?"

"I don't mean I get it, get it in the sense that I've experienced that, but it's a lot to handle. Have you talked to a therapist?"

I let out a sigh, thinking it said something about Graham that he had enough life experience to ask that. "Yeah. She said this is normal, and it's about figuring out how to deal with it."

"How did Alice handle your reaction?"

"I didn't really give her a chance. I left and came here."

"Oh, and worked out like the devil was chasing you." Graham's tone was dry as dead grass.

I could at least chuckle at that. That tight sense of panic that morphed into anger this morning had loosened in my chest, and I could breathe a little easier.

"Seems like Alice might be important to you," Graham observed, yet again proving he could be more perceptive than I preferred.

I was in deep with Alice. I loved her, and that couldn't last.

That afternoon, I stopped in to check on my grandmother. My parents were there, along with Dennis.

"How are you?" Gram asked, leaning up to press a kiss on my cheek.

I smiled down at her, kissing her cheek in return. "Doing all right," I replied noncommittally.

"Your parents are going back to Seattle for the week. Your father needs to take care of a few loose ends, and then he'll be back until I go," she said, way too matter-of-factly for my sanity.

My heart burned. "Do you have to be so casual about it?"

"It's not casual. It's reality. I am glad they'll be here until I go."

My father rolled his eyes when I glanced over. I knew how much he loved her, so I knew this hurt him, but he tended to rely on dry sarcasm to get through clutch moments like this.

"When do you leave?" I asked him.

"We decided this on short notice just this morning. We'll check on things at the house, I'll stop by the university, and then we'll come back."

"If you need the cabin, obviously, it's yours for the week," my mother offered.

My grandmother was feeling nosy about Alice and looked over at me curiously. I ignored her.

"Ah, well, I'll check with Alice, but I might use the place for the week. That gives her some privacy."

Later, I took the cowardly way out and texted Alice while I knew she was still at the clinic. *My parents are heading back for a week. I'll be at the cabin.*

I intended to figure out other arrangements before she returned because I had to find a way to get back on stable emotional footing. I needed to fall out of love with her, which didn't seem likely. I was relieved Honey was at the clinic with her when I swung by her house to get my things.

Chapter Thirty-Five

ALICE

I reread Jonah's text at the clinic. My heart hurt, and I wanted to cry. I didn't know exactly what happened to him this morning, but something had happened between his nightmare the night before and his reaction when he realized who was on the phone with me. I wanted to beat down his door and demand he explain, but I knew that wouldn't work.

"Hey, want to come with me tonight?" Tiffany asked, breaking into my train of thought.

"Where?" I asked.

"Card night."

"Uh, sure," I said. "Can I bring Honey?"

"Of course. Let's just go from here. You can feed her here. Conveniently, we have plenty of dog food," she teased. She paused before she turned away, her eyes coasting over my face. "Are you okay?"

Of course, she had to go and pick up on the fact that I was upset. I simply told her the truth because I knew Tiffany well enough to know she'd drag it out of me if I didn't. "Jonah was weird this morning. I guess his parents are returning to Seattle for the week, so he's going back to the cabin for the week."

She studied me quietly for a few beats before pushing from the doorway and wrapping me in a quick hug. She stepped back, resting her hands on my shoulders and squeezing firmly as she looked into my eyes. "It will be okay." She nodded in emphasis.

"You sure about that?"

"Of course, I am," she said. "Jonah will come around."

"You say that as if you know all of his secrets."

Tiffany's hands fell away from my shoulders, and she rested one on her hip. "Well, I definitely don't know all his secrets. I know he was in a school shooting, which has to leave an impact."

I sighed. "Of course. I only wish I understood what's happening now."

Chapter Thirty-Six

ALICE

I glanced around the table, marveling a little at everyone here. Having been back home for a while now, I'd seen almost everyone here in passing, but it was strange to be together with them. They had announced this was a no-kids night after we arrived. Beck, who I had known in high school as the biggest flirt in Willow Brook and potentially in the world, had appeared to cart off not one, not two, but three toddler-age kids. He was a family man through and through.

Maisie, his wife, smiled over at me as she shuffled the cards. "Do you have a preference for what game we play?"

I shrugged. "Not at all. Are we really playing cards?"

Amelia grinned. "Don't forget: Maisie will win."

"Oh right. This is where we all lose a little money," I teased.

"We don't bet more than five dollars," Maisie offered with a wink.

Holly waggled her eyebrows as she looked over at

me. "Maisie usually wins, or Lucy, or me. Are you up for beating one of us tonight?"

"Just consider that you have five extra dollars to win because I'm here," I offered.

We got started playing, and the conversation flowed easily. I promptly learned that if I wanted to get caught up on the gossip around town, I needed to come to card night with these women. We were all within a few years of each other in high school, and some I knew better than others.

Maisie had won two rounds when I glanced around the table, commenting, "It's really good to be home."

Maisie glanced up, her warm brown eyes twinkling as she smiled at me. "Willow Brook is the only place I've ever felt at home."

Phoebe, who happened to be seated to one side of me, curled her arm around my shoulders and gave me a squeeze. "And it's good for you to be home."

Madison caught my eye, offering, "I've fallen in love with Willow Brook. I don't know that I could've appreciated it when I was growing up, but I love how people take care of each other here."

"They do," I agreed.

Someone got up to refill the plates of appetizers. Tiffany nudged me on the side where she was seated. "Don't forget you can have as much wine as you want."

Paisley, who I had met tonight and was married to Russell, an old friend from high school, grinned. "You must be driving, Tiffany," she said dryly.

"Absolutely. Alice needs to relax tonight. She needs a brain break."

Holly glanced over, casting me what appeared to be nothing more than a polite smile. "So what's the scoop with you and Jonah? Alex told me he's been staying with you because his parents are staying in his place."

Amelia glanced at Holly, shaking her head slowly. "You've been sitting on that question, haven't you?"

"We've only been here an hour," Holly protested.

My cheeks were hot as I laughed. "It's fine. He was staying with me, but his parents are headed back to Seattle for a week, so he's back at his place."

"How very neighborly of you to let him stay with you," Madison offered.

"Well," I began with a shrug, feeling the heat burn a little hotter in my cheeks, "I wasn't about to say no when his grandmother asked me."

"How is Bea?" Susannah asked.

"I wish I knew. She had an episode where she was at the hospital for a night. She doesn't talk much about it. Her prognosis isn't good, even if she decided to do another round of treatment. She says she doesn't want to feel miserable."

"Chemo can be miserable," Holly offered. "Even younger people have a really hard time with it sometimes. I don't blame her for making that choice." Her smile was tinged with sadness. "She's a spark plug, though. She was a riot while she was in the hospital."

My heart stung a little just thinking about the uncertainty of how long Bea may be with us.

"How is Jonah holding up with that?" Phoebe asked.

"Okay, I think. I think he's resigned to it, for lack of a better way to describe it," I offered.

Susannah returned, placing two more plates of appetizers in the center of the table. Someone had picked up the variety platters to go from Wildlands, so we had various flavors of chicken wings, fried halibut bites, sliders, and more. I reached for one of the honey teriyaki wings and a chicken slider.

After a moment, Holly asked, "So what *is* the deal with you and Jonah? Bea mentioned she saw you two kissing."

I groaned, taking a bite of a slider and chewing, willing my embarrassment to dissipate. After a moment, I glanced over, offering, "Bea is nosy."

"So is Holly," Lucy commented dryly from her side.

That elicited a snort of laughter from Amelia. Holly merely shrugged, unabashed. "I don't care. I am nosy. Jonah is cute."

"And you're married," Maisie interjected.

"And whipped as far as I can tell," Susannah chimed in.

Holly threw her head back with a laugh. "So what? I have eyes. I'm just curious. I like Jonah. He's got that whole broody vibe going for him."

I felt protective of him. "Maybe so, but he's a really nice guy."

Tiffany snorted.

"What do you know?" Holly pressed.

Tiffany cast me a sly smile.

I rolled my eyes. "Fine. We were kind of having a fling. I think it's over."

"Oh no! It can't be over," Holly insisted.

"I'm not so sure that's your call," Susannah interjected.

"I think maybe with everything he went through, a relationship isn't the best choice for him right now," I replied.

Maisie met my eyes, understanding contained there. "Or maybe it's exactly what he needs. Something to remind him it's worth it."

"How do *you* feel, though?" Phoebe asked.

I hadn't come here tonight thinking I would spill my guts, but I did. I told them the plain truth—I was afraid I had fallen in love with Jonah.

After some back-and-forth, the group consensus was I needed to give him a chance. After Tiffany dropped me off, I walked down to the lake with Honey. It was cold tonight, and the frost on the grass crunchèd under my feet. Moonlight glittered on the surface of the lake.

I sat down on the end of the dock, wrapping my arms around my knees and resting my chin on them as I looked out over the lake. This was my place, the spot I'd always come to when I was younger, sometimes just because I wanted to be here and other times because I needed to think. I was abruptly struck with a rush of grief for my parents.

Even though they were gone, I still knew I was lucky. Because they'd loved me, and they'd loved each other. I knew not everyone got that in childhood. The loss was still sharp. From time to time, it sideswiped me out of nowhere. The first few years after they died, I avoided coming home. Everything was too emotionally loaded. I'd felt bombarded by memories. Yet slowly, the grief had felt less huge in my heart. Now that I was home, even though I came because I felt I had no other options, I was glad.

A bitter laugh slipped out. I contemplated calling Tyler to thank him for being an asshole. He hadn't called me again, and I was relieved.

It was good to be here, good to see old friends and make some new friends. Phoebe's question repeated in my thoughts. *How do you feel, though?*

I'd gone and fallen in love with Jonah. Like an idiot.

"Not what I planned," I murmured to myself.

I straightened and reached over to scratch behind Honey's ears. She propped her chin on my knee as I petted her.

I didn't know how Jonah felt. We didn't talk about our feelings. We just acted on them. What was supposed to be just sex had turned into so much more. He had almost seemed, well, not like himself this morning.

Every time I thought about his nightmares, sadness rolled through me, and my heart twisted sharply. I knew he hated them for obvious reasons. I just wished I could make it better for him. I sensed he didn't think love was a possibility for him. I loved him, but I loved him enough to want that for him regardless of whether I was the one he loved.

Honey nudged my leg. My hand had stilled on the back of her neck, and I smiled down at her. "I'm slacking," I teased.

She rolled over, and I stroked her belly. As I walked back up the dock a little while later, I saw a single light on in Jonah's cabin.

Chapter Thirty-Seven

JONAH

"What have you gone and done?" Gram asked, one hand on her hip as she wagged a spatula at me.

"Nothing," I insisted.

Her eyebrows hitched up. "I don't believe you. I know you, and you're lying."

"Geez, Gram. Cut me a little slack, would you?"

She shook her head as she lowered the spatula and turned to check on the omelet she was making. She flipped it and adjusted the flame under the pan. Turning back, she cocked her head to the side.

"We've all been giving you slack," she said gently. "What you went through is something no one should have to go through. Oh sure, tragedy happens and accidents happen. But this kind of thing, where someone shows up and guns down kids in a high school. We're failing." She paused, studying me for a moment. "And, I know you don't like how people view you as a hero for helping save the kids you could. I know you don't even think it matters. But it does. You did all you could in a horrible situation."

"I know," I whispered hoarsely as my heartbeat

sped. Whenever this topic came up, I felt a little sick, and my heart raced unsteadily.

"But that wasn't my point," she said, her sharp gaze skating over my face. "Your parents have been worried sick. I have too. We're all tiptoeing around you. Don't take that the wrong way. You're not being angry and explosive. But we're treating you like you're more fragile than you are. Do you want to turtle up and never let anyone in? I already know you love Alice. I've seen the way you look at her."

My mouth fell open while my heartbeat stuttered and lunged. I snapped my mouth shut.

"I'm going to stop tiptoeing around. You can get over this. The world is filled with people learning to live with the scars in their hearts. You're doing a disservice to those who died by swearing off loving anyone."

I stared at her. I wanted to argue, but her words hit me like a brick in my chest. Emotion tightened around my throat, forcing me to take a slow breath. My grandmother wasn't done yet.

"I love you, Jonah. You're my only grandson and therefore my favorite, but you also deserve to be my favorite." My lips tugged into a smile. It was a rueful smile, tinged with joy because I was a lucky kid. My parents loved me, and I had a grandmother who still spoiled me rotten. She loved me the hard way, not the easy way. To my point: this conversation.

"I don't know how you're going to figure this out. I know you saw a therapist for a while, so maybe you should call them again. Sure, I was teasing when I said I wanted you and Alice to be together. I'm also nosy, and I enjoy playing matchmaker. But having seen you two together, I actually think you're good for each other. Alice is steady and practical, and you need that.

I can't believe I'm about to say this, but she's probably smarter than you." I snorted at that. "So before you plan to shut her out, just know I will know from the grave if you do that." She wagged the spatula in emphasis.

"From the grave?" I couldn't help but prompt.

She turned off the burner and carefully slid the spatula under the omelet before flipping it onto a plate. "Yep. I'm not above a little guilt. I'm dying, and I know you'll miss me."

Those words felt like a lance through my heart, the pain sharp. I took a breath, nodding.

"So be a smart man and listen to me. Figure out your shit and let yourself love someone or, more specifically, love Alice. I know you already love her, but you're getting in your own way." She clucked as she handed me the plate. "Now, go sit down and eat."

Chapter Thirty-Eight

JONAH

I finished showering and got dressed. We'd just returned from dealing with a late-season fire. Like most of the West, Alaska was getting drier by the year, so the fire season stretched longer. In this case, some hikers had thought it was safe to camp and have a fire in an area where campfires weren't allowed. Shocker, but they started a forest fire.

Fortunately, an early snow moved in and helped us tamp it out quickly. It had been a tiring few days, and we had to camp in the cold.

I was just sitting down on the bench to lace up my boots when Graham appeared in the doorway to the locker room.

"Oh good, you're still here," he began.

"What's up?"

"Holly called from the hospital. Your grandmother's there."

My stomach felt hollow. "Oh shit," I muttered. I quickly laced my boots and stood, grabbing my jacket out of my locker and pocketing my keys. "Did she tell you anything else?" I asked as I walked toward the doorway.

Graham nodded. "She's stable, but Holly thought you'd want to know right away. She asked if your parents were back yet," he added as he turned and walked with me down the hallway toward the back door that led to the parking area.

I glanced at my watch. "They're due in tomorrow morning. I'll call them on my way over to the hospital."

"Do you want company?" he asked as he held the door open for me.

I paused, glancing over at him. "No, but thanks."

Graham dipped his chin in acknowledgment. "Call or text if you need anything."

I hustled over to my truck, definitely speeding on my way over. Fortunately, it was a short distance to the hospital, and I knew every cop in this town. The police shared the other half of our station, so we saw each other often. They might pull me over, but I figured they'd let it slide if they knew I was on the way to see my grandmother.

Alice feathered along the edges of my thoughts before strolling boldly in. I missed her. I still hadn't acted on my grandmother's comments last week. My heart rolled in an unsteady beat. I knew my grandmother was right. I did love Alice. It's just —

It's just, what? my critical mind queried sharply.

You're scared.

My thoughts flashed to the day of the shooting. The blood smeared on the floor, and all my thoughts centered on keeping the kids safe. Through the rush of adrenaline and trying to bottle my grief down with four of them dying right in front of me and then learning Tina had died at the very start. She was the first victim, according to the police. The only blessing I could dredge out of that brutal, devastating detail was that she hadn't had to endure it and worry.

I was cut up inside over her death and the kids dying. Tina and I had gone on a whopping total of four dates at that point. I'd liked her and thought maybe it would go somewhere. Then like the cut of a blade slicing through time, she was dead.

Alice is alive, a voice I rarely listened to chimed in, the tone a deep baritone.

My heart kept on beating. I felt like I was falling inside—as if I'd stumbled over the edge of a cliff and hurtled through the air. I didn't know what could break my fall.

No matter what, you already love her. You can't undo that.

I gave my head a hard shake and brought my thoughts back to Gram as I turned onto the road that led to the hospital. Of course, all thoughts that led to Gram also led to Alice because I knew exactly what Gram thought. She thought I was being a coward, even if she didn't say it like that.

Well, she has a point, my critical side offered up with a shrug.

My chest felt tight as if there were a band around it. I thought about Graham asking if I wanted company. The only company I wanted was Alice.

I abruptly remembered as I was pulling in to park that I had meant to call my parents. I snagged my phone out of the cupholder in the console, thinking I would call on my way in. I reconsidered, thinking it would be better to wait and call when I knew what was happening. Once I knew my grandmother was okay, I would find Alice.

Moments later, after I'd been directed to the

waiting area, Holly came striding in. "There you are!" she exclaimed.

I stood from the chair, commenting, "I asked for you when I got here. They said you were busy. How's Gram?"

Holly took a breath, letting it out quickly. "She's going to be fine. But not for long. You know we're just marking time."

Sadness gusted through me, a fierce and cold wind. "I know. What happened?"

"It's not because she's dehydrated this time. She slipped and fell. You know they got her shower all set up with supports and everything, but she really should be using her shower chair."

I rolled my eyes. "She hates that thing."

Holly shrugged. "I'm sure she doesn't like falling. Come on back." She gestured for me to follow as she turned. We walked out of the waiting area, down one hallway and then another before she led me into a room, offering, "She's already besties with her roommate."

I chuckled. "Of course she is."

"Hey, Gram," I said as we entered the room.

She smiled over at me. She was propped up on a ton of pillows and looked completely fine. She gestured toward the woman in the bed to her side. "This is Callie. We're almost up to speed on everything."

I glanced at Callie. "Nice to meet you. I'm Jonah." I thumbed toward my grandmother. "Her grandson."

Callie, who looked a little tired, glanced up with a smile. "Nice to meet you." Her voice was wispy. Frail as she was, she looked as if a gust of wind could blow her right out of her hospital bed. She looked over toward my grandmother. "If you want some privacy, you can pull the curtain closed."

Holly snorted. "Bea will have you over at her house after you're both out of here. Although, if you'd like things to be a little more private for yourself, just say the word."

Callie shook her head. "Oh, no need. It's nice to have visitors."

Between my grandmother and Holly, I had all the details about Gram falling in the shower within a few minutes. "She's lucky she didn't break a hip," Holly said, sliding a stern look in my grandmother's direction.

Gram simply rolled her eyes as she looked over at me. "I hate my bath chair."

"Oh, they're not too bad," Callie offered. "I was a little too proud to use mine at first, but now I can just sit down when I'm showering. It really is more comfortable, and you don't have to worry about falling."

"Listen to her," I said, looking back toward Gram.

She let out an elaborate sigh before adjusting the blanket over her hips. "Fine. I'll start using mine. Only because I don't want to come back here for being stupid. I absolutely hate giving people a reason to tell me that they told me so."

Holly tapped a few keys on the keyboard on the rolling cart beside Gram's hospital bed before standing and resting both hands on her hips as she looked down. "You're here for the night because we need to make sure you don't have any swelling. In the meantime, I will be here until midnight, so if you need anything, you know how to use the buzzer." She looked over toward Callie. "If she talks your ear off too much, just tell her to shut up."

Gram giggled while Callie smiled. After Holly departed, I sat down in the chair between their beds. "Is Dennis back out at the house?"

Gram nodded. "He is. He's making us dinner and bringing it in," she said in a conspiratorial whisper-shout.

"I don't think it needs to be a secret," I replied.

We chatted casually for a bit before calling my parents and giving them the update. After we took care of that, my grandmother looked from me to Callie. "Tell him what you told me."

"About what?" Callie countered.

"About being alone."

"Oh," Callie said slowly. She looked over at me. "After my first husband passed, my first love, who—" She paused before shrugging. "Well, life just happened, and it didn't work out when we were younger. He got in touch with me. He wanted to try again. Because we were both widowed." She shook her head. "And I was just feeling all too bitter about life. You see, my Johnny was sick for a long time, and I didn't want to lose somebody again." She picked at her blanket, adjusting it as she looked down. When her eyes lifted to mine again, there was a sheen of tears in them. "Then he died too, and I realized that was stupid. Sure, I have my children, but they're living their lives. I'm mostly alone, just bouncing around that house. I wish I hadn't passed up the time I could've had with him."

"I was telling her that I don't have an update from you on Alice yet, and I'm worried you're going to be stubborn," my grandmother interjected.

That band around my chest tightened. It felt as if a fist was squeezing my heart. "Gram, I have thought about what you said. I'm going to talk to Alice. I just haven't had a chance yet. You do know I've been out at a fire the past few days."

"You had almost a week before that," she offered pointedly.

I rolled my eyes. "I'm working on it."

"Well, you'd best. Because you love that girl. I might have to withhold my caramel brownies if you don't stop being stupid."

"Oh my, those sound delicious," Callie chimed in.

"When we're both out of here, you'll have to come out for a visit. I will send you home with a batch."

"They are as good as they sound," I offered.

After chatting with them for a while longer, I left to let them enjoy their dinner with Dennis. I was starving, but I needed some time with my thoughts and to muster up the nerve to talk to Alice. I decided to swing by the grocery store because I knew pickings were slim in my refrigerator. As I walked through with a cart, I caught sight of Alice by the deli. She was turning into the short hallway that led to the bathrooms. I hurried over with my cart and parked it beside the deli case, leaving it there as I sprinted down the hallway.

Chapter Thirty-Nine

JONAH

"Alice!" I called just before she turned the corner in the hallway.

The soles of her shoes squeaked on the tiled floor as she stopped, turning back to face me. My legs kept moving before I abruptly stopped several feet away from her. We stared at each other, the distance between us echoing with a force of emotion, need, and startling clarity. For me, at least.

Alice was still waiting, her eyes locked on mine.

I moved, taking three strides to close the space between us. I reached for her hands, curling both of mine around hers. A tremor ran through her, and my own body vibrated, such was my need to touch her. A sense of relief washed through me, like water let loose from a dam, the force initially overwhelming and then slowing.

"I miss you," I murmured, my voice coming out hoarse.

Her eyes blinked up at me. She was quiet, long enough that I began to worry that I had misread everything I felt between us, everything I thought I sensed from her in return.

She swallowed, her shoulders rising abruptly with a quick breath. My thumb brushed along the inside of one of her wrists, and I could feel the wild patter of her pulse there.

"I miss you too," she finally said.

I hadn't even noticed I was holding my breath until it came out in a whoosh.

"Gram's in the hospital."

"I heard. Holly texted me. She said she was going to be okay. I was going to stop by on my way home."

"I just came from there. She's doing fine. She's best friends with her roommate."

Alice's lips curled in a slow smile, her eyes softening as she looked up at me. "Of course, she is. How are you?"

My lips twisted to the side as I shrugged. "She's okay for now, but she's still dying, and that breaks my heart," I said honestly.

Alice squeezed my hands, releasing one and lifting her palm to trail her fingertips along the stubbled edge of my jawline. "I know. It breaks my heart too. How else are you?" she asked gently.

Something softened in my chest, the bands of tension that had been there since the day I watched four students die, and felt the collective adrenaline and fear pumping through everyone that afternoon. I took a quick breath as a tingling sensation spread through my body.

"I'm okay. I missed you. Before you, I thought I would never let anybody matter except the people who already mattered. But I love you, and I can't change that. I can't undo it. I miss you too much even though you're right next door. I know I can just walk through the trees, and you'll be there. Honestly, I think I might be an asshole when I'm not doing well."

Alice's palm slid down the curve of my neck to rest just over my heart. She pressed her palm firmly against me. My heart felt as if it were leaning forward into her touch. As if it recognized the essence of her as if my heart knew it would be safe in her capable, practical hands.

"I suppose we're all stumbling on this path called life."

"I didn't mean to leave so abruptly."

She tilted her head to the side, her eyes studying me quietly. "I understand. We could have a code word."

My brows rose as I cocked my head to the side, puzzled. "What do you mean?"

"A word when you just need to kind of not talk about what's going on and take a walk or whatever."

I chuckled. "I think maybe I need to deal better. You don't exactly crowd me to begin with." My heart kept beating, and the warmth of her palm above it comforted me.

Alice took one step closer, leaning up to press a kiss in the divot at the base of my throat. The heat of that touch rippled, sending sparks leaping across the surface of my skin.

I released her other hand, lifting mine to cup her cheeks as I bent low and brought my mouth to hers. She made this little sound at the back of her throat. It was subtle, but it snapped through my awareness, sizzling through my system. Her mouth opened on a whimper, and her tongue darted out to tease against mine.

I forgot where we were and spun her, pressing her back to the wall. My hands flattened against it as we kissed, the intensity of it too much as if she was a live wire. I needed to contain myself, to ground myself with the touch of the cool wall against my palms.

Our kiss deepened, and I pressed closer, feeling the sharp peaks of her nipples against my chest. I was hard, my arousal swollen and achy as I rocked into the cradle of her hips, the heat of her right there.

A sound broke through my awareness, and I abruptly remembered where we were—in the hallway at the grocery store with two public restrooms beside us. I lifted my head, stepping back just as someone came around the corner in the hallway. A woman walked swiftly past us. I glanced sideways to see her shaking her head and muttering something under her breath as she pushed through one of the doorways to the restrooms.

Alice giggled, dipping her head and tucking it into my shoulder. I slipped one arm around her waist and the other sliding through her hair as I held her close, laughing with her.

Chapter Forty

ALICE

That night, after we ate take-out pizza because we both abandoned our plans for grocery shopping, and after I fed Honey, the three of us walked together through the chilly darkness. With the stars bright and glittering in the crisp night and our breath misting in the air, Jonah's fingers laced through mine, and he tugged me toward the dock.

"Let's walk down here. Honey won't jump in, will she?" he asked, his voice low and clear in the quiet surroundings.

"She's decided the water's too cold."

"Smart girl." He laughed softly.

Moments later, we were standing at the end of the dock. Honey sat down, alertly looking out over the water where the moonlight rippled on the surface. Her eyes tracked the sound of a raven calling somewhere along the lake's shoreline.

Jonah turned to face me, reaching for my other hand.

"What is it?" I peered up at him.

"I thought since this is where we met, or met for

the second time," he corrected, and I smiled. "This was the perfect place to tell you something."

My heartbeat kicked faster, my belly flipping as anticipation fluttered through me.

"I never planned to fall in love with anyone, but I love you."

Tears stung my eyes, and my throat felt thick. "I love you too," I whispered.

On the heels of a breath, we were kissing. Honey circled our legs, her claws clicking on the wooden slats of the dock.

Back in the house later, Jonah mapped my body with his hands and lips. I held his eyes as he rose above me, my legs curling around his hips when he filled me with a deep thrust.

My climax broke over me in wave after wave as I cried his name, hearing mine in return when he shuddered above me. He held me close as we fell asleep.

EPILOGUE

Jonah

Six weeks later

"For once, you're doing things on schedule," Gram announced with her hands on her hips as she smiled up at me.

I chuckled. My heart felt so full my chest almost hurt. "We wanted you here for this," I said sincerely.

A month after Alice and I reunited, I asked her to marry me. Gram's presence at our wedding was deeply important to me. And not just because it would make her happy. My heart and soul knew it was important for her to see us off.

Alice was on board. Since her parents weren't here to be part of the wedding, Gram would walk her down the aisle. Believe me when I say she was *absolutely* thrilled with that.

"Are you ready?" she prompted.

We were getting married in Alice's backyard. Gram had originally wanted the wedding to take place at her house but had acquiesced when I pointed out that it was important for Alice to honor her parents by having the wedding there. "The view's almost the same," she had pointed out to Gram.

"I'm ready."

"Well, then get out there." My grandmother practically chased me out of her house.

The anticipation humming through me had me shifting on my feet as I waited beside my father, who was my best man. It was a very chilly afternoon. We'd had a dusting of snow last week, and Thanksgiving wasn't far away. Termination dust had already fallen on the mountains.

This was Alaska, so everyone was happy to stand outside for a gorgeous late autumn, early winter wedding ceremony. When I saw Alice coming out on my grandmother's arm, wearing her mother's wedding dress under an open long coat, I couldn't help the smile. It was automatic.

I was still worried about anyone mattering too much. But if I could do this messy thing called life with anyone, it was Alice. She stopped in front of me.

My grandmother whisper-shouted, "She's all yours!"

When I said my vows, my heart kept beating, and I didn't stutter. Alice's eyes held mine, her gaze steady and filled with love and warmth.

A little while later, Janet sat beside us at one of the tables in Firehouse Café, her eyes twinkling with her smile. "I just knew you two were meant for each other."

"Did you really?" Alice prompted, a small smile teasing at the corners of her mouth.

Janet nodded firmly. "I did. The first time I saw you two together here. I didn't know how long it would take you to figure it out. You've made your grandmother very happy."

"That's not why I fell in love with Alice, but it's convenient," I offered with a grin.

Janet hurried away moments later, and Tiffany sat down beside us. "Good thing you two figured this shit out. And, can we all agree how handy it was that that whole bullshit thing sorted itself out in time?"

The bullshit thing Tiffany was referencing was the legal case with the guy who'd been trying to blackmail Alice and, apparently, a bunch of other women he worked with. Even though his father was a partial clinic owner, the other owners were furious about the embezzlement and the other legal charges. With those cases, he was looking at multiple felony charges at this point.

Alice shrugged. "I'm glad it's dealt with."

Her fingers were laced with mine, and I squeezed lightly. "We didn't want that hanging over us for this wedding."

Alice glanced at the clock. "You know we have to go soon."

"Why?" Tiffany asked.

"Because Honey's waiting at home, and she needs dinner," Alice explained.

"I can take her for the night," Tiffany said. "I can't believe you didn't even think to ask me about that."

Alice shook her head. "It wouldn't feel right. She adores Jonah, and she's family for us."

Tiffany nodded. "Proof we should all just marry the people our dogs love."

Alice bit her lip as she laughed. "I think it's a good measure. A dog's judgment is purer than human judgment."

Tiffany giggled. "I guess if I ever meet anyone, I'll ask Honey what she thinks."

———

Alice looked over at me that evening. We were on the couch with Honey curled up against my hip. "We could've had Tiffany take care of Honey," she offered.

I shook my head. "I agree with you. Plus, we're doing our honeymoon next spring anyway."

She shifted closer to me. "We could go sooner if you want."

"All I want is you. I don't care where we are."

Thank you for reading Alice & Jonah's story! Want a glimpse of the future for them? Join my newsletter to receive an exclusive scene.

Sign up here: https://BookHip.com/NRRMGNT

p.s. If you are already subscribed, you'll still be able to access the scene.

Up next in the Light My Fire Series is All It Takes.

Tiffany is all about love for everyone. Except her. Romance is a giant no-thank-you. She considers herself immune to men.

Until she nearly melts on the spot at the sight of Wes. Wes was the nerdy, smart guy in high school. Now, he's one smoking' hot firefighter.

Life gets seriously complicated when a little boy who needs a family brings them together.

Don't miss Wes & Tiffany's story - it's swoony, emotional & sweet!

Pre-order All It Takes - due out Jan 24, 2023!

For more swoony romance...

This Crazy Love kicks off the Swoon Series - small town southern romance with enough heat to melt you! Jackson & Shay's story is epic - swoon-worthy & intensely emotional. Jackson just happens to be Shay's brother's best friend. He's also *seriously* easy on the eyes. Shay has a past, the kind of past she would most definitely like to forget. Past or not, Jackson is about to rock her world. Don't miss their story! Free on all retailers!

Burn For Me is a second chance romance for the ages. Sexy firefighters? Check. Rugged men? Check. Wrapped up together? Check. Brave the fire in this hot, small-town romance. Amelia & Cade were high school sweethearts & then it all fell apart. When they cross paths again, it's epic - don't miss Cade's story! Free on all retailers!

For more small town romance, take a visit to Last Frontier Lodge in Diamond Creek. A sexy, alpha SEAL meets his match with a brainy heroine in Take Me Home. Marley is all brains & Gage is all brawn. Sparks fly when their worlds collide. Don't miss Gage & Marley's story!
Free on all retailers!

If sports romance lights your spark, check out The Play. Liam is a British footballer who falls for Olivia, his doctor. A twist of forbidden heats up this swoon-worthy & laugh-out-loud romance. Don't miss Liam & Olivia's story.
Free on all retailers!

FIND MY BOOKS

Thank you for reading With Every Breath! I hope you enjoyed the story. If so, you can help other readers find my books in a variety of ways.

1) Write a review!

2) Sign up for my newsletter, so you can receive information about upcoming new releases & receive a FREE copy of one of my books: http://jhcroixauthor.com/subscribe/

3) Like and follow my Amazon Author page at https://amazon.com/author/jhcroix

4) Follow me on Bookbub at https://www.bookbub.com/authors/j-h-croix

5) Follow me on Instagram at https://www.instagram.com/jhcroix/

6) Like my Facebook page at https://www.facebook.com/jhcroix

Visit my store to purchase ebooks & fun swag!
J.H. Croix Shop
Light My Fire Series
Wild With You
Hold Me Now
Only Ever Us
Fall For Me
Keep Me Close
With Every Breath
All It Takes - coming Jan 2023!
Dare With Me Series
Crash Into You
Evers & Afters
Come To Me
Back To Us
Take Me There
After We Fall
Swoon Series
This Crazy Love
Wait For Me
Break My Fall
Truly Madly Mine
Still Go Crazy
If We Dare
Steal My Heart
Into The Fire Series
Burn For Me
Slow Burn
Burn So Bad
Hot Mess
Burn So Good
Sweet Fire
Play With Fire
Melt With You
Burn For You

Crash & Burn

That Snowy Night

Brit Boys Sports Romance

The Play

Big Win

Out Of Bounds

Play Me

Naughty Wish

Diamond Creek Alaska Novels

When Love Comes

Follow Love

Love Unbroken

Love Untamed

Tumble Into Love

Christmas Nights

Last Frontier Lodge Novels

Take Me Home

Love at Last

Just This Once

Falling Fast

Stay With Me

When We Fall

Hold Me Close

Crazy For You

Just Us

ACKNOWLEDGMENTS

The first draft of this book was written months before the shooting tragedy in the US in Uvalde, Texas. There are tragic shootings here almost daily, but when they involve young children, they bring an additional layer of trauma and sadness to the world. I almost reconsidered, but I told myself my readers are accustomed to me writing about sensitive topics, and it would be okay.

All of that said, I still worried some might misinterpret why I wrote this story. My husband is a hunter and has hiked miles into the wilderness for hunting year after year. We had the occasional brown bear concerns during the years we lived in Alaska, so having a gun available for safety was part of our lives.

But, but, but... The senseless tragedies that are piling up in this country break my heart and leave me and many others feeling helpless and deeply concerned for the future. My intent was to share a story about a character who experienced first-hand the effects of these shootings. I hope I did so with sensitivity and care. This wasn't written to make a political statement. I believe the safety of children is above all of that. I hope our world changes for the better, and I only wish I knew how to make that happen.

To my readers: thank you for reading, thank you for loving my stories and characters.

Gracious thanks to my editor, and to Terri D. for carefully mining for the details I miss, and to my early readers for being the last set of eyes to find any tenacious errors hiding in my sentences.

Najla Qamber spun magic yet again with this cover. A shout out to the bloggers, bookstagrammers, and booktokers who share the love of romance stories.

Much gratitude to my assistant for helping me with so many things. A special shout out to Angi H. for patiently helping me with my website and swag store.

As always, my husband and my dogs love me even when I'm writing too much.

xoxo
J.H. Croix

www.ingramcontent.com/pod-product-compliance
Lightning Source LLC
Chambersburg PA
CBHW061239210726